PRAISE FOR

the wisdom of hobbits

"Not since reading *The Tao of Pooh* so many years ago have I enjoyed a book of this nature as much as I did this one. It distills from a familiar body of fantasy literature invaluable insights to savor. Matthew J. Distefano shows through his close observation of Tolkien's Hobbits, in all their guileless homeliness and foibles, how wisdom and heroism are often disguised by the seemingly simple and insignificant. Although there is serious philosophy to be found in these pages (e.g., a discussion of faith and free will), Distefano wears his erudition lightly. Mostly, he wants us to recognize ourselves in these hairy-footed halflings and to learn from them. In short, this is a book about the adventure of living fully human lives, warts and all, and only superficially about Hobbits."

ADDISON HODGES HART
AUTHOR OF *THE OX-HERDER AND THE GOOD SHEPHERD: FINDING CHRIST ON THE BUDDHA'S PATH*

"The Hobbits of Tolkien's world are ready to guide you to your own wisdom through Matthew J. Distefano's expert care. Get out your travel map—or not—and get ready to explore the depths of the loveable, yet deceptively complex, Hobbits. For those yearning towards greater simplicity and connection with the world around them, grab this volume. It's time to settle in next to your fire and second breakfast for a delightful journey through Middle-earth—and you might just pick up some wise habits along the way."

REV. DR. KATY E. VALENTINE
ORDAINED MINISTER, NEW TESTAMENT
SCHOLAR, AND METAPHYSICAL ENGINEER

"The Shire, with its simple life and earnest people, offers wisdom for us wherever we live. Matthew J. Distefano distills that wisdom in this affable offering. After reading it, I'm planning new adventures—in the mundane of everyday life and the uncertainty of extraordinary times—and seeking a fellowship of travelers. Get this book and travel with me!"

THOMAS JAY OORD
AUTHOR OF *OPEN AND RELATIONAL THEOLOGY* AND MANY OTHER BOOKS

"A rare, balanced view of the oft-idealized Hobbits which shows how we can learn from both the good and bad of their culture, temperament, and way of life."

JOSHUA SCOTT
HOST OF *THE TOLKIEN LORE* PODCAST/YOUTUBE CHANNEL

"Matthew J. Distefano explores Middle-earth as loved by Hobbits, and like a master gardener he enumerates each flower of Hobbit perspective and personality in thoughtful detail. Then he relates the Hobbits' wisdom to the cares of the modern world, Hobbit to hobbit, heart to heart. Tolkien fans should love every word, right through to the appendices."

MICHAEL MARTINEZ
AUTHOR OF *UNDERSTANDING MIDDLE-EARTH:*
ESSAYS ON J.R.R. TOLKIEN'S MIDDLE-EARTH

"*The Wisdom of Hobbits* is a backstage pass to Middle-earth, where even minor characters have major roles in helping us understand that Hobbits are not just entertaining, they have lessons to teach us about the well-lived life. Matthew J. Distefano has opened Middle-earth in a way that will enthrall every Tolkien fan. Whether you can quote passages from *The Silmarillion* or just liked one or two of the films, this book will capture you and keep you reading. Distefano not only delights readers with a breathtaking knowledge of Middle-earth, he adeptly weaves in lessons to us, with their warnings, to the ways we choose to live in our world. From our personal interactions and opinions of friends and strangers to the way we choose to care for our environment, *The Wisdom of Hobbits* is an engaging way to learn and remember wonderful things about Hobbits and ourselves. This is a great book!"

BRIAN K. WOODSON, SR.
AUTHOR OF *PURPLYND*, SR. PASTOR, BAY
AREA CHRISTIAN CONNECTION

"Something that has struck me in my reading of Tolkien, rather beautifully, is the sense of ethics embedded in the text. Which has, of course, raised the question of if there are indeed any publications that might expound on such a thing. *The Wisdom of Hobbits* is such a book, encouraging its readers to learn from these stories and characters for all they are worth."

AARON DUNN
COMPOSER OF *THE SILMARILLION SYMPHONY*

"If you're a fan of J.R.R. Tolkien's works and looking for some inspiration in your everyday life, then *The Wisdom of Hobbits* by Matthew J. Distefano is a must-read. Matthew's passion for Tolkien's world shines through every carefully crafted sentence, and his unique ability to extract simple, meaningful wisdom from the complex plots and characters will help you feel grounded, alive, and ready to take on life's adventures with more grace and equanimity. As a therapist, I highly recommend this book for its therapeutic value. Don't miss out on this opportunity to discover the timeless wisdom of Hobbits and Middle-earth."

MARK KARRIS
LICENSED THERAPIST AND AUTHOR OF *RELIGIOUS REFUGEES: (DE)CONSTRUCTING TOWARD SPIRITUAL AND EMOTIONAL HEALING*

"What a gift, so many years after reading and re-reading and loving Tolkien's great work, to re-encounter it in such relevant ways to my life and values and deep questions. I loved getting to connect with how to engage community and overcome fear and show up well in hard times, all through my favorite characters in Middle-earth, Hobbits. Plus, the images and quotes kept me feeling immersed in that world in ways that made me feel like I was enjoying an escape even while I was learning valuable lessons along the way."

SANDHYA JHA
AUTHOR OF *THE LIBERATING LOVE DEVOTIONAL,
365 LOVE NOTES FROM GOD*

"'It is impossible to be both very rich and very good,' said Plato. Aristotle devoted fully a fifth of his highly technical and academic ethical treatise to the virtues only made possible through deep and abiding friendships. Matthew J. Distefano describes how good Hobbits work to balance these and other virtues into a well-lived life—not a life free from suffering, but a life *freed* to be good. Don't have time to read all of Plato and Aristotle? Then read Matthew's delightful little book distilling the wisdom of Hobbits into something more manageable."

RIC MACHUGA
PROFESSOR EMERITUS, BUTTE COLLEGE, AND AUTHOR OF
THE STORY OF CHRISTIANITY TOLD AS GOOD NEWS FOR ALL

"I had no idea what I was getting myself into when I opened this inspiring little book about Hobbit life. Matthew J. Distefano had me taking notes on how to live more fully in the present, which led me to reach out to a long-lost friend from the sixth grade to reminisce about the days of old—there was singing, laughter, and tears—and I am forever grateful. From ordinary life in the Shire to heroic adventures beyond, there is so much to be learned from the extraordinary lives of our Hobbit friends."

KAREN SHOCK
AUTHOR OF *TOO MUCH AND NOT ENOUGH*
AND COLUMNIST FOR PATHEOS

"As someone whose knowledge of Hobbits doesn't extend far past the Shire, I didn't expect to find the beauty, wisdom, and commonality between our lives to be so invigorating. The way Matthew is able to take you on an adventure through Middle-earth, uncovering the abundance of wisdom hobbits embody, while also weaving our lives as 'big folk' into their existence, will leave you ready to embrace life's next great adventure, as well as finding the balance and joy in the in-between."

LACI BEAN
CERTIFIED TRAUMA RECOVERY COACH

"As a foreigner to J.R.R. Tolkien's world of myth and magic, *The Wisdom of Hobbits* serves as the perfect tour guide into the life and mind of Tolkien's most endearing characters. From the savory selections of pipe-weed to the sacred nature of the simple life, Matthew J. Distefano's unique ability to both educate and engage serves as his very own Mathom, his gift of enlightenment to each reader. I cannot think of a better way to experience the wonder of Middle-earth than to embrace the beautiful present moment that is Distefano's *The Wisdom of Hobbits*."

DESIMBER ROSE
AUTHOR OF *THE CHURCH CAN GO TO HELL* AND
COHOST OF THE *HERETIC HAPPY HOUR* PODCAST

the wisdom of hobbits

*Unearthing our Humanity
at 3 Bagshot Row*

MATTHEW J. DISTEFANO

Copyright © 2023 by Matthew J. Distefano

First Edition

Cover design and layout by Rafael Polendo (polendo.net)
Bilbo Hand font by Nancy Lorenz (nancylorenz.com/lothlorien/)

ISBN 978-1-957007-38-0

This volume is printed on acid free paper and meets ANSI Z39.48 standards.

Printed in the United States of America

Published by Quoir
Chico, California

www.quoir.com

table of contents

PART I: HOBBIT WONDER

PART II: HOBBIT WILL

PART III: HOBBIT WISDOM

foreword

The wife of a colleague of mine once rhetorically and sarcastically asked, "So, *The Lord of the Rings* is basically about a bunch of people running around in the woods?" As if that is a bad thing. Most stories are too complicated anyway, and are about things that don't matter. Does anyone honestly like *Inception*? My favorite books and movies are simple. *The Martian*, for example, is about an astronaut trapped on Mars, trying to get home. Simple. *The Edge* is about three guys (eventually two) being chased around the Alaskan wilds by a Kodiak bear.

But simple does not mean shallow. No, the plot of *The Lord of the Rings* isn't complicated. And sure, a Philistine could say Frodo was *merely* trying to get from point A to point B. But one could argue the depth of the nature of sacrifice—a theme throughout *The Lord of the Rings* (and beautifully discussed by Matthew)—is contained within "running around in the woods." And let me say this: I never got around to caring about what happened to Dom Cobb, the protagonist of *Inception*. I was too busy trying to figure out what on earth was going on. Don't get me wrong, it was a clever movie, if not ultimately shallow. On the other hand, I care deeply about Sam and Frodo. The simplicity of the narrative gives room for Tolkien to explore the things in life that matter—friendship, sacrifice, the seductive and corruptive nature of power, the joys of good tilled earth, et cetera.

Simplicity is honest. Eat, sleep, defecate, procreate: that is all life is, according to the *X-Files* (even if we like to kid ourselves it isn't). So, embrace the simplicity! It turns out Hobbits know what's what. The fact is tomatoes grown from your garden are more delicious than store bought, and your fancy, high-paying job doesn't mean much at all (I'm looking at you, Saruman).

Having known Matthew for going on a decade now, I can guarantee that in every way but stature, he is a legitimate Hobbit—especially when it comes to friendship. We started hanging out around the time of my coming of age (thirty-three), and at that point, relationships had me jaded. The fact is that most people move away, or aren't willing to put in the effort needed to maintain a meaningful friendship. So, imagine my surprise when I stumbled upon someone who genuinely cared for me and was invested in my life. To this day, it is embarrassing how much I lag behind his skills in friendship. It is always Matthew who initiates playdates. It is always Matthew who gives the more thoughtful gifts—typical of a true Hobbit.

He is also a lover of things that grow. I wish I could take full credit for the beauty of my backyard, but alas, I cannot. Anytime I get a compliment about such things, I have to sheepishly say, "Uh, yeah, Matt did that." While I can honestly claim the awesomeness of my wood pile, the orchard, massive garden, and burgeoning vineyard are all his doing.

Furthermore, he is fond of ale and pipe-weed. In fact, if I remember correctly, it was the Southfarthing's finest that we originally bonded over. To my utter dismay, we have had to scale back our trips to The

Green Dragon, if you follow me, given we are both advancing in years (well past our coming of age). But it is better to have loved and lost. Regardless, our bonfire sessions—the natural culmination of our decadent, Hobbit ways—are still a thing to behold: a big, bright fire, the feel of a pipe in your hand, epic conversation, and copious amounts of chips and salsa. Oh, and Leonard Cohen playing in the background.

I consider nights like these, along with the universe's other gifts, to be the point of life. Why else am I going to work? It is not out of the goodness of my heart, that's for sure. I have heard of people cultivating their careers because they find them rewarding, but I am not one of them. I work because I have to; but I would always—*always*—rather be relaxing. That is not to say I don't see the value of hard work—work is a necessary part of the work/relax cycle. But it seems more correct to say we work in order to make our relaxation rewarding, than to say we relax to be more productive at work. To each his own, I suppose. I am confident a Hobbit would agree with me.

And finally, Matthew knows a lot about Tolkien. Maybe too much. I would pit his knowledge against the biggest of nerds, maybe even Stephen Colbert … so, clearly you can trust what he has to say throughout this wonderful little book.

— **Michael Machuga**
November 10, 2022
Paradise, California

pRɛʄꜗqce

For my entire adult life, I have been enamored with all the goings on in Middle-earth. From the sheer scope and size of *The Lord of the Rings* and *The Silmarillion*, to the way in which J.R.R. Tolkien uses prose to describe the world he so painstakingly but lovingly created, everything about Middle-earth fascinates me.

Though I have a love and appreciation for Elves, Dwarves, and Men, nothing piques my interest or tugs at my heartstrings more than Hobbits. A quick glance at me and you'd have to conclude that I could never be counted among them; I am quite tall, slender yet fairly muscular, and don't have hairy feet (though they sometimes end up on the table). I do not particularly like social gatherings, am not enamored with gift-giving (though according to Michael am quite adept at it), nor do I look forward to my own birthday party. However, where I miss the mark in terms of stature and social prowess, I more than make up for in my ability to smoke from a pipe and tend to a garden. Like Tolkien, it is in these qualities where I am a Hobbit in all but size.[1]

I am also a writer, though not to the same degree as Tolkien. I have yet to create a world of fiction, and will never create my own mythologies or languages. However, where I lack in world building, I make up for in interpretation—in taking the works of others and teasing out the philosophical, ethical, and psychological truths contained therein.

That is where this project comes in.

Hobbits have so much wisdom to offer us, and my goal here is to elucidate for you just what those qualities are. If, at the end of reading this book, you desire to start living more like a Hobbit, then I will have done my job. If, in turn, living more like a Hobbit brings more peace, happiness, and contentment to your life (to your own personal Shire), that would make me more joyous than a Baggins stumbling upon a shortcut to mushrooms.

Of course, not everyone is as obsessed with Tolkien's world as I am. Others, like the many scholars and other aficionados to whom I read and listened to in preparation for this book, are perhaps even more so. The folks who deserve the most praise include Dr. Tom Shippey, Dr. Verlyn Flieger, Wayne Hammond and Christina Scull, Dr. Corey Olsen, Alan Sisto, and Shawn E. Marchese. With their scholarship in mind, as well as the many Tolkien books I have digested over the years, I will be tasked with the following: to strike a balance between

· · · · · · · · · · · · · · · · · · ·

1   Tolkien, *The Letters of J.R.R. Tolkien*, "Letter #213."

inundating my readers with random facts, dates, Tolkien quotes,[2] and footnotes, and glossing over the finer details of what it means to be a Hobbit. In other words, I want to refrain from scaring off casual Tolkien fans but also avoid embarrassing myself in front of any potential Tolkien scholars who may happen upon this book. All in all, there will no doubt be random facts about Hobbits, as well as a good deal of footnotes. But please don't think of this book as a detailed history of Middle-earth or even Hobbit lore. That is not the point here. The point will be twofold: To show you exactly why the wisdom of Hobbits is so meaningful, thereby inspiring you to apply what you've learned to your own life. The finer details of Hobbit tradition will just be there to bring color to the pages and strengthen the arguments I am attempting to make.

So, why write this book and why now?

It's simple, really. It's my heartfelt contention, based on forty years of existence, that Western culture has, by and large, fallen out of love with the simple life. We've taken for granted what makes us most grounded. We pass by people in the streets, never considering where they have come from or where they are going. We pass by produce in the stores and fail in many of the same ways. We think that we will find the most happiness on social media, doom-scrolling through our feeds without so much of an idea as to what, exactly, we are looking for. In short, we go through life on autopilot, never smelling

....

2   Throughout this book, I quote Tolkien a lot. The reason I do this is twofold: 1) it's my belief that in order to do justice to the topics at hand, we must look primarily to the source material (i.e., *The Hobbit, The Lord of the Rings, The Silmarillion*, Tolkien's letters, etc.), and 2) out of a deep respect and adoration for the author. I'll note that secondary material is also used quite a bit, but not to the extent of the source material.

the nasturtians,[3] or noticing the singing thrushes, or feeling the cool autumn breeze on our faces.

In applying the wisdom of Hobbits, however, we will start recognizing these things more frequently. We'll recognize our need to connect with the earth, our need to go on an adventure, our need to have a comfortable bed to come home to when our bodies get weary, and perhaps most importantly, our need for fine fellowship among fellow Hobbits. With the help of Bilbo, Frodo, Sam, Merry, Pippin, the Gaffer, Elanor, Farmers Maggot and Cotton, and others, we will begin to slow down, to appreciate the sights, sounds, tastes, feelings, and smells of everything around us. As we reflect on the stories of Hobbits both great and small, we will start to acknowledge that perhaps we've been too hasty throughout our lives. As we put into practice the things we discover, we will no doubt find ourselves living a more peaceful life, connected to the earth, full of awareness and presence, and replete with an appreciation for even the seemingly mundane aspects of it.

That is my hope, anyway. It is my hope that the wisdom of Hobbits can be applied in a universal way, and that by doing so, we will start to become more connected to the earth and each other. But if not, then the words of Gandalf, wise as they are, give me great comfort, and take away some of the pressure I have put on myself to do more than my

. . . .

3   For those who aren't aware, the nasturtian was the subject of a disagreement between Tolkien and a proofreader for *The Fellowship of the Ring*. This poor fellow corrected Professor Tolkien's "nasturtian" to its now more commonly spelled "nasturtium," apparently not realizing that the nasturtium is a type of watercress, while the nasturtian is a popular garden flower found in Bag End. With its red, orange, and gold flowers, it was and still is a favorite among gardeners. Needless to say, the correction was retracted, and Tolkien's preferred spelling now appears in the text.

part in altering our course. I leave them with you now, in hopes they can bring you comfort as well:

> It is not our part to master all the tides of the world, but to do what is in us for the succour of those years wherein we are set, uprooting the evil in the fields that we know, so that those who live after may have clean earth to till. What weather they shall have is not ours to rule.[4]

. . . .

4 Tolkien, *The Return of the King*, 160.

acknowledgements

As a Hobbit in all but size, I resonate most with Samwise Gamgee, mainly because of our shared love of things that grow. That would mean my wife Lyndsay is Rosie Cotton (minus the furry feet), as she is the most beautiful Hobbit in all the Land (partly because she doesn't have furry feet). I have her to thank for too much to write here.

Unlike Rosie and Sam, we only have one daughter: Elyse. She is an inspiration and a motivation, and is growing up to be a wonderful young woman—one as brave as Éowyn and as beautiful as Arwen.

Michael Machuga is my best friend and has coauthored a whole host of books with me. If I am Sam, then he is Mr. Frodo. Nothing is better than sitting on his porch, smoking from a pipe, and looking over our orchard and garden.

I can't thank Rafael and Teighlor Polendo enough for what they have done with and for Quoir Publishing. Years ago, when they were just a young startup, something deep inside me said to submit a manuscript to them, and to this day, it is the best professional decision I ever made.

To everyone involved with the Heretic Happy Hour podcast: thank you. I don't know how we've made it this far, but I'm so glad that we have.

Michelle Collins, my friend, confidant, and fitness inspiration, has been beyond a blessing to me. I'm so thankful she is in my life.

A huge shout out to my content editing and proofreading team: Jason Elam, Brandi Elam, Crystal Kuld, Greg Kuld, Karl Hand, Tim Higgins, and Cameron Horsburgh. This book would have never looked so good without your help.

A warm "thank you" is owed to all the Tolkien geeks, nerds, and scholars who have continued to keep J.R.R. Tolkien's work alive and growing well past his earthly life. From the fine folks at The Tolkien Society to the talented team at The Prancing Pony Podcast—even Old Butterbur—and everyone in between, you have done the Good Professor a great service.

And to everyone else too numerous to name—from my former editors and Patreon supporters, to my wonderful launch team, to everyone who reads my books and blogs—I can't thank you enough. Like when Sam carried Frodo up the side of Mt. Doom, you have kept me going when I felt as if I could go no further.

author's note
A Word About the Cover and Subtitle

I f you have a keen eye and a broad knowledge of Hobbit lore, you may have noticed an apparent discrepancy between the hobbit-hole on the cover and the address in the subtitle. For those who are not aware of what in Eru's name I am talking about, allow me to explain.

The home on the cover, being that it has a green door, represents Bag End, the hobbit-hole we most associate with Bilbo and Frodo Baggins. However, the subtitle includes "3 Bagshot Row," which is home to Samwise Gamgee.

So, why the apparent discrepancy?

Simple.

The apparent discrepancy represents just how much Sam changes and adapts during the events of *The Lord of the Rings*. "3 Bagshot Row" is his home at the beginning of the story, when he is bashful, shy, and unsure of himself. But it is also his address during the time in which he grows the most. That growth is represented by Bag End, the home Frodo gifts him prior to departing for the Undying Lands. Bag End is represented on the cover, then, because it's where Sam ends up, but only by becoming an extraordinary Hobbit during his residence at 3 Bagshot Row.

introduction

"Hobbits are an unobtrusive but very ancient people, more numerous formerly than they are today; for they love peace and quiet and good tilled earth: a well-ordered and well-farmed countryside was their favorite haunt."[5]

— FROM THE PROLOGUE TO *THE FELLOWSHIP OF THE RING*

Hobbits are a fascinating bunch. They generally enjoy the simple life—gardening, eating, drinking ale, eating some more, and smoking the finest pipe-weed they can get their hands on. For most, these modest pleasures are all that are needed to enjoy their time in Middle-earth. Others, however, need something more. They need

. . . .

5   Tolkien, *The Fellowship of the Ring*, 1.

adventure. They need to see mountains, and Elves, and Dwarves, and even Ents.

This is true for the most famous of Hobbits—Bilbo Baggins and his nephew Frodo—but it is also true of many others, including the always adventurous Took family. As the story goes, it was Old Took's great-grand-uncle, Bandobras "Bullroarer" Took, who led the Hobbits in the Battle of Greenfields after goblins from the Misty Mountains invaded the Northfarthing. Legend has it that Bandobras even killed the chief goblin, Golfimbul, by knocking his head off with one swing, sending it flying a hundred yards and down into a rabbit hole.[6] As simple as Hobbits may at first seem, there is something within them that deserves a more thorough investigation. To quote Gandalf: "Hobbits really are amazing creatures [...] You can learn all that there is to know about their ways in a month, and yet after a hundred years they can still surprise you at a pinch."[7]

Nothing truer could ever be said. Hobbit ways are simple—some would even consider them dull and dimwitted—yet they will surprise you decades after your first meeting. Their land is simple—some would even consider it unkempt and unruly—yet, if you are truly paying attention, its beauty will warm your heart the moment you step foot in it, as well as years after leaving it. That is one reason we continue to keep coming back to our furry-footed friends; they keep having more and more to show us.

Throughout this book, we will explore the many ways Hobbits model how to live happy and contented lives. From lessons about

. . . .

6   Tolkien, *The Hobbit*, 18. This is said to be how
     the game of golf was invented.

7   Tolkien, *The Fellowship of the Ring*, 69.

becoming one with the earth, to learning how to rebuild after tragedy, there will be much to learn.

But does that mean Hobbits are perfect? By no means. As we'll soon discover, they can certainly be myopic and sheltered, as well as rather xenophobic, even to their own kind.[8] For instance, right at the beginning of *The Fellowship of the Ring*, we witness this very thing:

> "But what about this Frodo that lives with him?" asked Old Noakes of Bywater. "Baggins is his name, but he's more than half a Brandybuck, they say. It beats me why any Baggins of Hobbiton should go looking for a wife away there in Buckland, where folks are so queer."[9]

Not wanting to be outdone in the gossiping and besmirching of other Hobbits, the Gaffer's next door neighbor chimes in with,

> "And no wonder they're queer," put in Daddy Twofoot, "if they live on the wrong side of the Brandywine River, and right agin the Old Forest. That's a dark bad place, if half the tales be true.[10]

This conversation goes on for some time, which goes to show one thing: Hobbits, while charming, like all other races of Middle-earth, are also complicated. Yes, they can be quite extraordinary in their resolve, able to resist both Sauron and the power of the Ring more so than any other race (except, of course, for Tom Bombadil,

....

8 I say this, not as a slight, but as a truth about all races of Middle-earth. Hobbits are no more xenophobic than other races, including Elves (see, for instance, *The Silmarillion*, pp 195–98, where Thingol, the Elven King of Doriath, shows great malice toward men, especially Beren, his daughter Lúthien's beloved. In fact, Thingol is said to not include any from the race of Men in his service).

9 Tolkien, *The Fellowship of the Ring*, 22–23.

10 Ibid., 23.

whatever race he happens to be—if race is even the correct term for such an enigma). But they can also be trivial and petty, ostracizing and demonizing those whom they really know little about. Incidentally, this juxtaposition is exactly what makes them perfect models for us Big Folk, as we are often quite similar in our ways.

Of course, I am not saying we humans should emulate the worst of Hobbit behavior. I am saying quite the opposite, in fact. Because Hobbits are complicated, able to perform the most heroic of tasks, yet sometimes so simple-minded that they cannot even speak well of people who live a mere fifty miles away, they make the perfect case study for us—we who are often quite similar in our disposition. To that end, our task will then be to take the good from Hobbits, learn from their shortcomings, and hopefully discover how we can then apply this knowledge to live more peaceful and fruitful lives, connected to each other and the world around us.

A BRIEF HISTORY OF HOBBITS

Naturally, most of us associate Hobbits with the Shire, but their history goes back prior to establishing these roots. Though their *exact* origins are unknown, Hobbits trace their history to the northern regions of Middle-earth and below the Vales of Anduin.[11] At the beginning of the Third Age—the Age in which both *The Hobbit* and *The Lord of the Rings* take place—Hobbits emigrated west and north, possibly due to the growing danger in Greenwood (what would later become known

....

11   The Vales of Anduin are the fertile valleys adjacent to the Anduin
      River. They extend for hundreds of miles, and lay between the
      Misty Mountains to the west and Mirkwood to the east.

as Mirkwood). They settled in Bree-land, Dunland, and the Angle between the rivers Hoarwell and Loudwater.

It's not until hundreds of years later when they would settle what would eventually be known as the Shire. In 1601 of the Third Age, two brothers, Fallohides called Marcho and Blanco, led a large group of Hobbits further west, across the Brandywine River, and onto its western banks. After the Battle of Fornost in T.A. 1975, which ended the kingdom of Arthedain[12]—the kingdom that oversaw the region that included the Shire—the Hobbits, no longer under the rule of a king, elected their first Thain (military and diplomatic leader). Though the office of Thain would quickly come to be seen as nothing but a formality—after all, Hobbits have always led extraordinarily peaceful and uneventful lives—it represented the unofficial founding of "The Hobbits of the Shire."

The first Thain was called Bucca of the Marish, but after his family headed east, back over the Brandywine River, in order to settle what would come to be known as Buckland, a new Thain, from a new family lineage, had to be selected. This new line came from the Took family (of which Peregrin Took, aka "Pippin," traces his lineage), and this is how Pippin became a prominent and important Hobbit.

While the Thain is, in one sense, significant, the position holds no real power in the Shire. The real power, if we can even call it that, comes from the office of Mayor of Michel Delving. Located in the

....

12   Arthedain was one of three realms of the Dúnedain, created after
the kingdom of Arnor split in T.A. 861. It lasted until T.A. 1974,
when the Witch-king captured the capital of Fornost, driving out
most of the Dúnedain. After the kingdom of Arthedain came to
an end, the lands remained largely empty, save for the Shire and
a few other towns and settlements. Its people became Rangers,
of which Aragorn, the future king of Gondor, was one.

White Downs, Michel Delving is the Shire's largest town and center of all "government" operations, including Postmaster and First Shirriff (the Shire's de facto police force). The position of Mayor is usually elected, though sometimes has had a history of being handed down through birthright. They serve for seven years, and there are no official limits to how many terms the Mayor of Michel Delving can serve.

After the events of *The War of the Ring*, Samwise Gamgee will be elected Mayor and will serve for seven consecutive seven-year terms. Other prominent mayors throughout history include Will Whitfoot and Frodo Baggins (who will act as Deputy Mayor for roughly six months while Mayor Whitfoot recovers from his imprisonment at the hands of Saruman and Lotho Sackville-Baggins—*more on that later*).

THREE TYPES OF HOBBITS

FALLOHIDES

The Fallohides, though the least common type of Hobbit, were the first to cross the Brandywine River and settle the Shire. They typically have fair skin and hair, and are taller and more slender than other varieties of Hobbit. They enjoy hunting and are on friendly terms with Elves, which is perhaps one reason why they have always been so gifted with language and music.

STOORS

The Stoors, unlike the Fallohides, were the most reluctant to emigrate west. They have always preferred living in the flat lands, typically near water. Whereas the Fallohides are tall and lean, Stoors are generally broad and stout, possessing large hands and feet. As a note, prior to becoming known as Gollum, Sméagol was a Stoorish Hobbit, living near the Anduin River.

HARFOOTS

When we think of Hobbits, we imagine Harfoots: smaller and shorter than all the others, possessing browner skin, unable to grow a beard, and never seen wearing any boots or shoes. They were the first to start building their homes in the side of hills, and are typically skilled with their hands and feet.

AGE & APPEARANCE

Though Hobbits are counted among the Atani—the race of Men, created by Ilúvatar—they generally live longer than the Big Folk. Their average lifespan is about 100 years, but many live even longer than that. (Merry, for instance, dies at 109, while Pippin dies at 101. Sam and Frodo, if you'll recall, will leave for the Undying Lands after the events of *The War of the Ring*.) For the Hobbit, middle aged is roughly fifty years. The fact that Frodo is fifty-one years old when he first leaves the Shire at the beginning of *The Fellowship of the Ring* should come as no surprise.

As to their appearance, in Tolkien's essay "Of Dwarves and Men," he explicitly states that although Hobbits are "of very short stature," they are "in nearly all respects normal Men."[13] However, they do have round, jovial faces, slightly pointed ears (like those of Elves), and furry

. . . .

13   Tolkien, "Of Dwarves and Men," from *The Peoples of Middle-earth*.

feet with leathery soles (which is why they don't need to wear shoes).[14] As we'll see in the next section, however, culturally they are distinct in a few ways.

HOBBIT CULTURE

As we discussed earlier, Hobbits enjoy the simple life—farming and gardening, lots and lots of food, the brewing (and especially the drinking of) ales, throwing parties and giving gifts, and the smoking of pipe-weed. They are often suspicious of those they call "outsiders," which often just means anyone not from their immediate locale. Unlike the Big Folk, Hobbits rarely desire power and prestige, which is one of the main reasons they can resist the Ring better than their larger counterparts.

Some Hobbits live in hobbit-holes, or "smials." Others live in low buildings such as Brandy Hall. But nearly every building in the Shire, whether burrowed into the ground or built on top of it, has round doors and windows.

Birthdays are especially grand occasions, where gifts are given to others rather than received. As such, presents are often regifted throughout the Shire. In fact, Hobbits keep to this practice so much so that they developed a term for it: Mathom.

PIPE-WEED

A part of Hobbit culture that deserves its own section is the smoking of pipe-weed. While many might call it a habit, Hobbits call it an

. . . .

14   Tolkien, "Letter #27," from *The Letters of J.R.R. Tolkien.*

art.[15] Where this artform came from is anyone's guess. In Meriadoc Brandybuck's *Herblore of the Shire*, he states, "When Hobbits first began to smoke is not known, all the legends and family histories take it for granted."[16] What isn't taken for granted, Merry continues, is when pipe-weed crops are first grown in the Shire, and by whom; it was around the year 1070 of the Shire Reckoning[17] (2670 of the Third Age) by Tobold Hornblower of Longbottom—in the Southfarthing.

While Hobbits are almost synonymous with the smoking of pipe-weed, they weren't the ones responsible for introducing the crop to Middle-earth. That honor goes to the Númenóreans, who allegedly brought it from Númenor sometime during the Second Age. Hobbits are, however, the first to plant it in their gardens. For the people of Númenor and Gondor, it is a weed that either goes by the name *Sweet Galenas* or Westman's-weed, depending upon who you ask.

Arguably the best pipe-weed is grown in the Shire's Southfarthing. There are three varieties grown there: Longbottom Leaf, Old Toby, and Southern Star. In Bree, a variety called Southlinch is grown, but according to Barliman Butterbur (the innkeeper at The Prancing Pony), it is nowhere near as good as anything grown in the Southfarthing.[18] According to Bilbo, Old Toby is the best variety, while Merry and Pippin favor Longbottom Leaf.

. . . .

15 Tolkien, *The Fellowship of the Ring*, 9.

16 Ibid.

17 The Shire Reckoning is the calendar used by Hobbits. It began when the Shire first became colonized in 1601 of the Third Age. Like the calendar used by Men, Dwarves, and Elves, it has twelve months, but differs in that each month has thirty days, with five extra days being devoted to special festivals.

18 Tolkien, *The Return of the King*, 293.

HOBBIT WISDOM

Now that we've established some basic historical facts about Hobbits, their customs, and general practices—likes and dislikes—we can move on to the wisdom they can impart on us bigger people. Because, Hobbits are not just charming Shire-folk who dress in bright colors like yellow and green, halflings who like tobacco and mushrooms—though these things *are* true—Hobbits are imbued with knowledge and insights into the world which can help us lead happier, more contented lives. From balancing the need for a home and an adventure, to drawing closer to the earth on which we live, to understanding how our wills can live in alignment with Ilúvatar, wisdom is there to be found. Not everything, however, will be quaint and charming. Hobbits have suffered much. From having their homes torn apart by Saruman and the Dunlendings (ferocious men fighting under Saruman's command), to dying by the thousands during the Days of Dearth,[19] to having to flee to the Undying Lands after living through the events of *The Lord of the Rings* (including a pierce from a Morgul blade), Hobbits have endured much. And yet, they have done just that—endured. Through it all, they've kept their resolve, and have shown bravery in the midst of great evil.

This Hobbit tenacity has not gone unnoticed, which is why we are still talking about them so many decades after the release of *The Hobbit* and *The Lord of the Rings*. Peaceful, yet surprisingly ambitious, small, yet shockingly sturdy, Hobbits carry all the tools necessary for showing us how we can become better versions of ourselves, no

....

19   The Days of Dearth were a five-month period of extremely cold weather—lasting from November T.A. 2758 to March T.A. 2759—which led to the death of thousands of Hobbits.

matter where our place is in the world. Indeed, if we pay close enough attention, Hobbits can help us create our own little shires wherever we are—at peace, connected to the earth, and always appreciative of good food, fine friends, and great fellowship.

So please, put your proud, furry feet up, grab a comfortable seat next to the fire, fill your favorite pipe with the Southfarthing's finest, pour a glass of Old Winyards, and settle in for a satisfyingly whimsical yet philosophical look into what it means to live as a Hobbit.

"It is no bad thing to celebrate a simple life."
— BILBO BAGGINS

PART 1

hobbit wonder

A Hobbit is an adventure,
A Hobbit is a home.
Though they suffer stormy weather,
A Hobbit is never alone.

an adventure and a home

"I should like to save the Shire, if I could—though there have been times when I thought the inhabitants too stupid and dull for words, and have felt that an earthquake or an invasion of dragons might be good for them. But I don't feel like that now. I feel that as long as the Shire lies behind, safe and comfortable, I shall find wandering more bearable: I shall know that somewhere there is a firm foothold, even if my feet cannot stand there again."[20]

— FRODO BAGGINS, FROM "THE SHADOW OF THE PAST," IN *THE FELLOWSHIP OF THE RING*

The average Hobbit detests adventures. "Nasty disturbing uncomfortable things!" says Bilbo Baggins. "Make you late for

....

dinner!"[21] Of course, this is said the minute Gandalf arrives in the Shire for the first time since Old Took died; before Dwalin, Balin, Kili, Fili, Dori, Nori, Ori, Óin, Glóin, Bifur, Bofur, Bombur, and Thorin show up at his door looking for a worthy thief to help them in their Dwarven quest;[22] before his run in with the three Stone trolls in Eriador; before being captured by Goblins near Goblin-town; before his chance encounter with Gollum on an island in the middle of a dark, hidden lake deep within the heart of the Misty Mountains; and before his face-to-face meeting with the dragon Smaug under the Lonely Mountain. In other words, Bilbo hated adventures before ever embarking on one, the way children hate eating their vegetables before ever taking their first bite.

After his quest with the Dwarves, however, Bilbo changes his tune. When Gandalf shows up years later, this time to celebrate Bilbo's eleventy-first birthday, Bilbo admits, "I want to see mountains again, Gandalf—*mountains*; and then find somewhere where I can *rest*."[23] Of course, at this point, Bilbo is old, "well-preserved" as it were. So, he certainly isn't looking for the type of adventure he had over a half a century prior. He is, however, looking for something *different*—something far removed from his home at the end of Bagshot Row, where relatives are always prying around, and strings of confounding visitors never stop ringing his bell.[24]

....

21 Tolkien, *The Hobbit*, 4.

22 *The Hobbit* begins with a group of Dwarves seeking a thief to help them find a buried treasure that lies under a mountain guarded by the dragon Smaug.

23 Tolkien, *The Fellowship of the Ring*, 34.

24 Ibid.

What Bilbo realizes, over the course of his long, storied life, is that to be content in this world is to strike a balance between going on an adventure, and being safe and cozy in your hole in the ground. And by "hole in the ground," we are not talking about a "nasty, dirty, wet hole, filled with the ends of worms and an oozy smell, nor yet a dry, bare, sandy hole with nothing in it to sit down on or to eat," but a "hobbit-hole, and that means comfort."[25] In fact, this hole—this *home*—is the epitome of comfort. Like all hobbit-holes, it has a round door; Bilbo's is painted green and has a yellow brass knob in the middle. Inside, it has lengthy tunnels, with bedrooms, bathrooms, cellars, plenty of pantries, multiple wardrobes, kitchens, and dining rooms sprawling throughout.[26] The walls are paneled, the floors tiled and carpeted, and there are plenty of hooks and pegs for hats and coats—Bilbo has always loved hosting guests. On the left side of the home are the windows, which overlook his gardens and the meadows beyond. Off in the near distance is The Water, where the Party Tree has stood proudly for many long decades. Across The Water is the mill and the iconic Green Dragon Inn, which is nestled between Bywater and neighboring Hobbiton.

This is the home that, originally, Bilbo can't imagine leaving but, eventually, can't leave quickly enough. So, what happens in between these two meetings with Gandalf? Simply put: he sees the world, and it is bigger and more wondrous than he ever could have imagined. It is full of peril, yes, but it is also full of mountains that reach far above the clouds, valleys and meadows that stretch farther than the eye can see, forests enchanted by elven *magic* (though they would never use

....

25   Tolkien, *The Hobbit*, 1.

26   For a detailed rendition of Bag End, see Appendix B, Figure 1.

such a word), and rivers and waterfalls and pools so clean you can see your reflection in them as if you are looking into a mirror. His home in the heart of the Shire is beautiful, no doubt; but the broader world is just as awe-inspiring. Once Bilbo understands that, he can never see things in the same way. He has to find a balance between an adventure and a home (or, in this instance, a hole in the ground).

DIGNITY TO TAKE A RISK

For Bilbo to discover life's balance—of having a home and going on an adventure—he needs to be afforded the dignity of taking a risk. He needs to be a Hobbit in charge of his own life, to be self-determined. Considering Bilbo is middle aged when he begins his journey to the Lonely Mountain, it is obvious that he should be afforded such dignity. Other Hobbits from Hobbiton *do* think it rather strange—they say as much at just about every opportunity—but it is not custom for anyone to step in and try to stop him. Folks in the Shire take care of their own affairs and government is limited if not out-and-out nonexistent. The only meddling that goes on consists of gossiping and telling tall tales, as well as the occasional young Hobbit stealing mushrooms from a certain local farmer.

As children, we are afforded such dignity in incremental ways. The younger we are, the less risk we are allowed to take. Perhaps we are allowed to run around Bilbo's birthday party until well past our bedtime, but nothing more. As we develop, we are granted more flexibility and freedom, even though there could be the risk of getting hurt. Maybe we wander too far from home and get caught by Farmer Maggot and his vicious dogs, or perhaps we have a run-in with Gandalf after trying to steal some fireworks. In instances such as these, we will often face harsher consequences, and may even get hurt in some way. But an argument could be made that the risk is well worth it. Maybe the mushrooms you discover are the best mushrooms you have ever tasted, or maybe the fireworks Gandalf brought this time are the biggest and most colorful any young Hobbit has ever seen. Either way, the point being: to live a balanced life, you need to have *some* sort of adventure, and to have any kind of adventure, you need to take *some* sort of risk. There really are no two ways about it.

WEIGHING THE RISK

The question then becomes: how do we weigh the risk? The answer, as is the case with most of life's big decisions, isn't always cut-and-dried, as it depends on several factors.

Sometimes life presents us with a choice like Bilbo's—to go on an adventure for the sake of adventuring. No doubt, if he and the Dwarves end up plundering the gold from the dragon Smaug, he will be rich beyond his wildest imagination; but this is not the main driving factor in pushing Bilbo over the edge. Here's how Tolkien describes it:

> As they sang the hobbit felt the love of beautiful things made by hands and by cunning and by magic moving through him, a fierce and jealous love, the desire of the hearts of Dwarves. Then something Tookish[27] woke up inside him, and he wished to go see the great mountains, and hear the pine-trees and the waterfalls, and explore the caves, and wear a sword instead of a walking-stick. He looked out of the window. The stars were out in a dark sky above the trees. He thought of the jewels of the Dwarves shining in dark caverns.[28]

. . . .

27   Bilbo's mother, Belladonna Took, comes from a long line of particularly adventurous Hobbits. Hence the term "Tookish."

28   Tolkien, *The Hobbit*, 15–16.

Bilbo leaves with the Dwarves the following morning, first and foremost, because he wants to experience something different. He has loved his home at Bag End and the gardens that adorned it. He has loved the Shire and all its rolling hills and sweeping meadows. I'm sure he has especially loved many a night spent at The Green Dragon, drinking ales, telling tales, eating good, plain food, and singing robust, jolly songs. But the call to see the wider world is far too great for Bilbo, so he decides to venture out. Even though he could suffer the worst—Thorin says as much when he admits that some, if not all, may never return[29]—Bilbo decides to go anyway. And even though some in fact do *not* return—Fili, Kili, and, sadly, even Thorin—Bilbo never shows any regret for having gone with them. He shows sadness, of course, for these Dwarves would become close friends, but never regret for having gone with them on their quest.

On the other hand, we have Frodo, who has little choice in the matter. Unlike Bilbo, who adventures for adventure's sake, Frodo's journey, roughly three-quarters of a century later, is essentially forced upon him. Though in the past he has talked a great deal about *perhaps someday* having an adventure, he has not foreseen the type of journey he would end up on.

I say "essentially" because, while Frodo's hand is practically forced, his will still has a part to play (which we'll discuss at length in chapter 6). While discussing how to destroy the Ring, Frodo initially suggests hammering or melting it.[30] This bemuses Gandalf, who challenges Frodo to try. Naturally—or better yet *unnaturally*—Frodo ends up not even feigning an attempt. Why? Because he is

. . . .

29   Ibid., 17.

30   Tolkien, *The Fellowship of the Ring*, 66.

already under its power: "Gandalf laughed grimly. 'You see? Already you too, Frodo, cannot easily let it go, nor will to damage it. And I could not 'make' you—except by force, which would break your mind.'"[31] The choice to destroy the Ring has to be Frodo's and Frodo's alone.

After explaining the only way the Ring could be destroyed, Frodo asks Gandalf to do it, for him to take up the call in Frodo's stead. Gandalf, being the wise wizard he is, refuses: "With that power I should have power too great and terrible. And over me the Ring would gain a power still greater and more deadly."[32] The only option, Gandalf admits, is for Frodo to make his decision.

After a long pause, Frodo finally concedes to do what he must. He acknowledges that while the Ring may cause him great harm, the sacrifice will be well worth it:

> "I cannot keep the Ring and stay here. I ought to leave Bag End, leave the Shire, leave everything and go away." He sighed [...] "Of course, I have sometimes thought of going away, but I imagined that as a kind of holiday, a series of adventures like Bilbo's or better, ending in peace. But this would mean exile, a flight from danger into danger, drawing it after me."[33]

This is the decision Gandalf wanted, even needed, Frodo to make (and perhaps knew he would make). So, he offers the following counsel:

> "The Ring will not be able to stay hidden in the Shire much longer; and for your own sake, as well as for others, you will have to go, and

. . . .

31   Ibid., 67.

32   Ibid.

33   Ibid., 68–69.

leave the name of Baggins behind you. That name will not be safe to have, outside the Shire or in the Wild. I will give you a travelling name now. When you go, go as Mr. Underhill."[34]

After this validation, Samwise Gamgee shows up. In a relatively short time, Frodo and he head off on what will become one of, if not *the* most epic adventures ever embarked on in Middle-earth's history. But to get there, choices have to be made. Frodo has to see the bigger picture, to see beyond himself, if he ever wants to save the Shire. Heartbreakingly, he realizes that he may never see the Shire again, that it may never be saved for him; but if he wants to save it for his fellow Hobbits, he knows what he must choose to do. So, he chooses it. Though he is afraid—"very small and very uprooted," as he puts it—he makes the decision to do what's right, according to his noble Hobbit heart.

WHICH HOBBIT WILL WE CHOOSE TO BE?

Throughout our time on this earth, we will most assuredly be confronted by adventures the same as both Frodo and Bilbo. At times, we will find ourselves rather bored with life, pondering what it would be like to take a risk and head out into the wide-open world. Other times, life will force itself upon us and we will have to act, as if we really don't have much choice in the matter. So, the question we will have to ask ourselves is *what will we do about it when these choices come our way?*

The first option would be to act just like Bilbo did when the Dwarves first knocked on his door. We can put our foot down and

. . . .

34   Ibid., 69.

say "No!" And you know what? Most times we won't be forced to do otherwise. Life may pass us by and our Dwarven friends will be on their way. But at what cost? Perhaps regret—regret that life has moved on without us as we remained comfortable in our cozy hole in the ground. Maybe guilt for the same reason. And I'm guessing even a bit of resentment and jealousy for those who *do* choose to step out their front door.

The second option will be to allow the Tookish side to well up in us, giving us courage to take a risk. As we have discussed, sometimes adventures will be presented to us in non-threatening ways, like they were for Bilbo. But at other times, we will have to decide to make a sacrifice for the betterment of our Hobbit friends, just as Frodo did. Either way, it's going to take a large dose of bravery and valor. Because as Bilbo used to say, "It's a dangerous business, Frodo, going out of your door. You step into the Road, and if you don't keep your feet, there is no knowing where you might be swept off to."[35]

As is the case with all things, however, we will inevitably fall into both camps at different periods in our lives. And that is okay. Sometimes we *do* need a holiday, but not a holiday away from our hole in the ground, a holiday in it. Life can be difficult, the Road perilous. If we adventure too often and for too long, never putting any roots down, we will burn out quicker than one of Gandalf's fireworks.

This is where we need to find balance.

....

35   Ibid., 82.

FINDING BALANCE

"People need balance. They need a home and an adventure [...] They need to know that even if the adventures of life go awry, they can always regroup around the firepit at home, so to speak."[36]

— Michael Machuga

The key to all of this is finding balance. How we find balance is by being present in the moment in front of us, not wobbling or wavering in our convictions. Sure, like both Bilbo and Frodo, we may struggle to make certain difficult decisions. But if we really lean into the present moment, the right decision will usually present itself to us quickly, as it did for both of our Hobbit friends. All we must do, as Gandalf reminded Frodo on the night he leaves the Shire, is "decide [...] what to do with the time that is given us."[37]

If you have spent any time being present in the "now"—not reconsidering the distant past or worrying about the potential future—you know how powerful presence is in giving us great insights into whether it is best to stay at home, tucked away in safety, or to venture out on some new adventure. It goes by many names—a gut feeling, our intuition—but ultimately both are the same. Whether the adventure presented to us is a new job opportunity, starting our own business, moving abroad, or going back to college, matters not. The point is that whatever the adventure may be, it will be something that takes you out of your comfort zone and onto the road less travelled. But as Treebeard reminds both Merry and Pippen, it's best not to be

. . . .

36   Distefano and Machuga, *The Bonfire Sessions*, 37.

37   Tolkien, *The Fellowship of the Ring*, 56.

too hasty. Not every adventure is right for us. Again, presence and self-awareness are crucial in finding our balance.

APPLYING THE WISDOM OF HOBBITS: FELLOWSHIP ABOVE ALL ELSE

One thing we haven't yet mentioned, but will be a theme throughout the entirety of this book, is the power of fellowship.[38] Bilbo experienced it with Gandalf and the Dwarves. Frodo experienced it, first with Gandalf and Sam, then with Merry and Pippin, and finally with the rest of the Fellowship of the Ring. This is of vital importance because it lightens our burdens. Whether we decide to stay home or head out on the Road, fellowship, in one form or another, is always needed.

If you will recall, Bilbo loved hosting guests at his home in Bag End. The sheer number of hooks and pegs for coats and hats was a testament to this fact. But he also loved adventuring with his Dwarven friends—maybe not at first, but eventually. Frodo, on the other hand, always loved Sam, though their bond *did* increase exponentially throughout their trek to Mordor. Without Sam, he would have never made it to Bree, let alone the cracks of Mt. Doom; our two Hobbit heroes needed friendship and fellowship (perhaps just as much as they needed fresh, clean water and dense lembas bread).[39]

....

38 I was tempted to devote an entire chapter to fellowship, but thought better of it, opting instead to weave the themes of friendship and fellowship throughout every chapter.

39 Lembas bread is a type of Elven bread made for travelling. It is said that one wafer could feed a man for a day. The members of the Fellowship of the Ring are given lembas by the Elves of Lothlórien after their stay in the Elven realm.

The same is true of us Big Folk. When we are at home, while it is nice to be alone for a time, it is always refreshing to be sitting around the hearth, chatting with likeminded loved ones. Drinking wine is wonderful, but sharing a bottle of Old Winyards with a fellow Hobbit is better yet. And who wants to smoke pipe-weed alone when you can sit on your porch with your best friend and stare out over your gardens and meadows?

During daring adventures, however, friendship and fellowship are even more needed. At times, we will weaken and that's when having others there to share the burden can be lifesaving. Think about the end of Frodo's journey. When he could no longer walk, Sam, in one of the most touching scenes throughout the entire tale, literally carries him up the final ascent, saying, "Come, Mr. Frodo! I can't carry it for you, but I can carry you and it as well. So up you get! Come on, Mr. Frodo dear! Sam will give you a ride. Just tell him where to go, and he'll go."[40]

Nowhere is the power of friendship and fellowship more evident than here. Having Sam by his side meant that leaving the Shire, perhaps to never step foot in it again, could at least be tolerable for Frodo. Because here's the truth of the matter: no matter how wonderous and beautiful and peaceful the Shire is, no matter how aesthetically beautiful its gardens and meadows and hills and rivers are, the Shire isn't just the land. The Shire is the inhabitants that live in the land. To put it as plainly as I can: *the Shire is a Hobbit*. It is fellowship and friendship, and whether cozied up near the fire in their holes in the ground, or taking the final ascent into the heart of Mt. Doom, the Shire was and will always be with both Frodo and

....

40   Tolkien, *The Return of the King*, 233.

Sam because both Frodo and Sam share in the struggle. So, it is for us as well! Whether we are curled up on the couch with our spouse and children, watching *The Lord of the Rings* for the thousandth time, or whether we are moving across the country to a place we've never visited, our home is found in the people we share our lives with, the ones we love and cherish, until the end of our days.

·· 2 ··

extraordinary hobbits

*"Then something Tookish woke up inside him, and he wished to go and
see the great mountains, and hear the pine-trees and the waterfalls, and
explore the caves, and wear a sword instead of a walking-stick."*[41]

— FROM "AN UNEXPECTED PARTY," IN *THE HOBBIT*

We concluded the previous chapter by rephrasing—albeit in a lengthy manner—the old adage, "Home is where the heart is." For Hobbits of both the Shire variety and those of us who are only halflings in spirit, this is especially true. While we find a good deal of comfort in a roaring fireplace, a spread of meats and cheeses

. . . .

41   Tolkien, *The Hobbit*, 15–16.

and fresh-baked breads, a soft mattress and pillow to rest our heads on, home is wherever we are surrounded by friends and fellowship. Without these, our holes in the ground, no matter how comfortable they are, are merely houses. It is in sharing these comforts with others that they transform into something more.

But what happens when Hobbits stay too close to home? What happens when they live as if the borders of the Shire *are* the borders of the world? That is what we will be exploring at the onset of this chapter, before we turn our attention to our group of extraordinary Hobbits who will help lead us out into the broader lands of Middle-earth.

AN INSULAR WORLDVIEW

"All that is gold does not glitter;
Not all those who wander are lost ..."[42]

— Gandalf

We explored some of this in the introduction, but it bears repeating; for all their charm and appeal, Hobbits have some shortcomings, one of which is their propensity to live insular lives. Many rarely travel outside the borders of their immediate village, let alone the borders

. . . .

42   Tolkien, *The Fellowship of the Ring*, 193.

of the Shire.[43] This causes them to view all outsiders as a danger and a threat, and even leads them to seeing their own people as such.

Take, for instance, a conversation between Old Noakes of Bywater, Daddy Twofoot, and the Gaffer, which takes place at The Ivy Bush prior to Bilbo's eleventy-first birthday party.[44] In this lengthy exchange, the three Hobbits hardly mince words; Old Noakes calls folks from Buckland "queer,"[45] Daddy Twofoot agrees and emphasizes that they live on the "wrong side of the Brandywine River," and even the Gaffer chimes in by reminding the others how unnatural it is for any Hobbit to use a boat.[46] He then goes on to say that those who live in Brandy

. . . .

43 As we discussed in the introduction, this is not true of Hobbits prior to the events of the mid to late Third Age. During what Hobbits call the Wandering Days, Hobbits travelled quite extensively due to the growing threat of Sauron in Dol Guldur. From the Vales of Anduin to the foothills of the Misty Mountains, on into various parts of Eriador and finally, what would become known as the Shire, the Hobbits during the 11th and 12th centuries T.A. wandered far and wide.

44 The Ivy Bush is a small inn on the Bywater Road, where the Gaffer, Old Noakes of Bywater, and Daddy Twofoot gossip and slander Hobbits who live outside of their immediate vicinity.

45 Tolkien's use of "queer" has nothing to do with sexuality or sexual orientation. Nor is it a slight against the gender and sexual minority community. As I point out in an article entitled "Reclaiming the Word 'Queer'," Tolkien uses the word to describe anything from "strange" Hobbits who live in distant parts of the Shire, to strange woods just outside of it. In fact, the word gets even more complex when we consider the Middle Low German usage, which has a context of spoiling the success of something—as in, the queer trees of the Old Forest spoiling the success of the Hobbits' journey through it.

46 Tolkien, *The Fellowship of the Ring*, 22–23.

Hall live in "a regular warren, by all accounts."[47] On the surface, this may not seem like much, but if we dig a little deeper (pun intended), there is perhaps a more sinister meaning. As Dr. Corey Olsen points out in his lecture on chapters 1–3 of *The Fellowship of the Ring*, the term "warren" may be a derogatory term in that it implies Hobbits from Buckland are less civilized, opting to live as wild rabbits would.[48]

In an ironic twist of fate, when Frodo, Sam, and Pippin arrive at Farmer Maggot's farm, the same language is used to describe Hobbits from Bywater and Hobbiton. This causes Sam to be quite uneasy and agitated. (It should be noted that while Farmer Maggot does not live in Buckland per se, being from the Marish, he identifies more with Bucklanders than Hobbits from the Shire proper.) Here's Maggot, giving Frodo some unsolicited, but not unbiased, advice:

> "I'll tell you what to think," said Maggot. "You should never have gone mixing yourself up with Hobbiton folk, Mr. Frodo. Folk are queer up there." Sam stirred in his chair, and looked at the farmer with an unfriendly eye. "But you were always a reckless lad. When I heard you had left the Brandybucks and gone off to that old Mr. Bilbo, I said that you were going to find trouble. Mark my words, this all comes of those strange doings of Mr. Bilbo's."[49]

Now, Maggot is not necessarily wrong. Frodo *does* get caught up in "trouble" because of Bilbo's adventures. After all, the Ring never

. . . .

47   Ibid., 24. Brandy Hall was a huge smial built by Gorhendad Oldbuck. It has "three large front-doors, many side-doors, and about a hundred windows." (Ibid., 110–11)

48   "The Lord of the Rings: The Fellowship of the Ring, Session 1–Hobbit Values." *Signum University.* (January 12, 2016.) https://youtu.be/0f9bQrQD8HA.

49   Tolkien, *The Fellowship of the Ring,* 106.

would have come to Frodo if Bilbo hadn't happened upon it while deep in the Misty Mountains. But as shrewd and wise as Maggot can at times be, that isn't necessarily relevant here. What *is* relevant is that no matter *what* goes on with Bilbo or any of the other Hobbits from Hobbiton, they are not to be trusted. This would have been the case whether Bilbo had answered the call to adventure with the Dwarves or not. To Maggot, every Hobbit from Bywater to Hobbiton (perhaps even including Michel Delving and elsewhere) is viewed as peculiar and outlandish, whereas Bucklanders and those nearby are culturally normative. As Maggot goes on to say, "I'm glad that you've had the sense to come back to Buckland. My advice is: stay there! And don't get mixed up with these outlandish folk."[50]

The distrust of outsiders only continues when Hobbits encounter non-Hobbits—Elves, Dwarves, Men, and even wizards. As Tolkien explicitly states in the Prologue to *The Fellowship of the Ring*, "Even in ancient days they were, as a rule, shy of the 'Big Folk,' as they called us, and now they avoid us with dismay and are becoming hard to find."[51] And when describing Gandalf, many of the Hobbits use the word "dratted."[52] Even Frodo, well after meeting Strider, later admits the following to Gandalf:

> "I have become very fond of Strider. Well, *fond* is not the right word. I mean he is dear to me; though he is strange, and grim at times. In fact, he reminds me often of you. I didn't know that any of the Big People were like that. I thought, well, that they were just big, and rather stupid: kind and stupid like Butterbur; or stupid and wicked

. . . .

50   Ibid.

51   Ibid., 1.

52   Ibid., 45.

like Bill Ferny. But then we don't know much about Men in the Shire, except perhaps the Breelanders."[53]

Frodo's ignorance at this point, indeed the entire Shire's ignorance, is on full display in that last sentence. He is admitting that while Hobbits don't know much about Men, they will certainly draw strong conclusions about them regardless. And yet, they are dead wrong, as Gandalf quickly points out: "you don't know much even about them, if you think old Butterbur is stupid [...] He is wise enough on his own ground."[54]

Up to this point, Frodo has only been gone for a month and a day, and yet—partly because of Gandalf's scolding—he has already learned so much. Before he began his quest, he presupposed other races to be dull, stupid like the innkeeper in Bree. But after a month of seeing the outside world—and a minute of talking to Gandalf—he has been forced to quickly reconsider his position. Butterbur is not stupid, as Gandalf reminds us. And Strider is someone whom they could trust, as they quickly find out. This just goes to show you that you should not make judgments about that which you know very little, not unless you desire to be made more foolish than a Took.[55]

. . . .

53   Ibid., 247.

54   Ibid.

55   I say this as a joke, and not a slight against Peregrin Took and his family. In fact, the Tooks, being the adventurous types, are more than likely much less closed off and xenophobic than other families from in and around the Shire.

HOBBITS FROM BREE

"For my hope was founded on a fat man in Bree; and my fear founded on the cunning of Sauron. But fat men who sell ale have many calls to answer; and the power of Sauron is still less than fear makes it."[56]

— Gandalf

Thus far, we have explored the ways in which Hobbits from the Shire proper and its immediate outlying areas distrusted anyone from outside their borders. But what about Hobbits that live *outside* the Shire? Certainly, they aren't as numerous as those who live within its borders, but they still exist. Take, for instance, the Hobbits from Bree.

Located east of the Shire and south of Fornost in Eriador, Bree is a village occupied by both Men and Hobbits. Being that it sits at the crossroads of the East-West Road and the Greenway, it is a rather cosmopolitan town. Folks from all over travel there, often staying at the Prancing Pony Inn. Dwarves, Men, Hobbits—all of them gather in one place, telling stories from their own towns and villages over pints of ale.

Because of this multicultural exposure, the Hobbits who live there often show curiosity toward strangers, rather than standoffishness. Here's how Tolkien describes the scene after Frodo, Sam, and Pippin arrive at the Inn (Merry had already taken leave and was outside getting some fresh air):

> The Bree-hobbits were, in fact, friendly and inquisitive, and Frodo soon found that some explanation of what he was doing would have to be given. He gave out that he was interested in history and geography (at which there was much wagging of heads, although

. . . .

56   Tolkien, *The Fellowship of the Ring*, 292.

neither of these words were much used in the Bree-dialect). He said that he was thinking of writing a book (at which there was silent astonishment), and that he and his friends wanted to collect information about hobbits living outside the Shire, especially in the eastern lands.

At this a chorus of voices broke out. If Frodo had really wanted to write a book, and had had many ears, he would have learned enough for several chapters in a few minutes.[57]

As the evening continues, drinks start flowing—they come in pints, you know!—and more stories are told. In fact, things become so comfortable between the Shire-hobbits and Breelanders that Pippin—being the fool of a Took he often proved himself to be—tells the story of Bilbo's magical birthday disappearance. This leads to a less than sober Frodo trying to distract the crowd by dancing and singing on the tables, which causes him to accidentally put on the Ring. And poof! Just like that, he too disappears before their eyes, just like Bilbo did back at the Shire some time ago. Of course, this is not wise or prudent, as they are supposed to keep a low profile; but what it reveals about both sets of Hobbits—the ones from the Shire as well as the ones from Bree—is that when their guards are let down, they really have much in common. They love drinking and eating and singing and telling stories, and all that talk about so-called outsiders being nothing but strange and untrustworthy is just nonsense.

. . . .

57   Ibid., 176.

INTO THE WILD

As our four companions travel farther and farther away from the Shire, they end up meeting more and more unique characters. This only proves, without a shadow of a doubt, that what they grew up hearing about "outsiders" is simply untrue. Elves aren't to be feared, as they are some of the fairest beings in all of Middle-earth. Here's how Tolkien describes Frodo's initial thoughts upon entering the hall of Elrond after his recovery from the Morgul blade: "Such loveliness in living things Frodo had never seen before nor imagined in his mind; and he was both surprised and abashed to find that he had a seat at Elrond's table among all these folk so high and fair."[58] And when Frodo sits down next to the Dwarf Glóin, he isn't met with anything but politeness. In fact, Glóin even assists Frodo in gathering up some cushions that Frodo has accidentally scattered in his haste.

It's not just the guests of honor in Rivendell who meet Frodo with kindheartedness and compassion, however. Later in the journey, well after the Fellowship has split and it is just Frodo and Sam (with Gollum in tow), they are confronted in Ithilien by Faramir, Captain of the White Tower. While their initial meeting isn't exactly cordial, it isn't hostile either. In fact, when Faramir discovers that Frodo is carrying the One Ring, and that his brother Boromir tried to take it to use it as a weapon for Gondor, Faramir remains true to his vow to not attempt to take it, thus proving his mettle. And when Gollum is spotted fishing in the Forbidden Pool next to Henneth Annûn—which was punishable by death—Faramir spares his life at the request of Frodo. Lastly, after Faramir bids them leave, he sends Frodo and Sam with full bellies and the promise to move freely throughout

....

58   Ibid., 253–54.

the land of Gondor. This again causes Frodo to acknowledge the compassion and friendship of those whom many Shire-hobbits would consider to be untrustworthy outsiders:

> "Most gracious host," said Frodo, "it was said to me by Elrond Halfelven that I should find friendship upon the way, secret and unlooked for. Certainly I looked for no such friendship as you have shown. To have found it turns evil to great good."[59]

All in all, as our four companions travel farther and farther away from the Shire, zig-zagging all throughout Middle-earth, they meet creatures great and small. Many of them end up being foes, but even more become friends. From the Breelanders who share drinks and laughs with the Hobbits, to the Elves in Rivendell and Lothlórien who adorn the Company with gifts and tidings, the more they travel, the more they find out just how wrong they have been in believing that folks who lived outside the Shire are nothing but strange and untrustworthy.

BECOMING EXTRAORDINARY

> "One thing I have learned about Hobbits: they are a most hardy folk."[60]

> — Aragorn

For our Hobbit friends, to become extraordinary is to meet new people who are not like they are. The same is true for all of us. If we stay insulated, away from everyone who leads different lives, we will

. . . .

59 Tolkien, *The Two Towers*, 342.

60 Jackson, *The Lord of the Rings: The Return of the King*.

inevitably end up like Old Noakes of Bywater, Daddy Twofoot, or the Gaffer—noble Hobbits in their own right, but judgmental, gossiping, and xenophobic at the same time. Worse yet, we may end up like Sandyman, the Miller of Hobbiton, or, Eru forbid, his son, Ted.

To avoid this fate, we must step outside our borders and meet new people—people of various races, religions, nationalities, genders, and sexual orientations. We must learn to trust them, to see them without prejudice, as fellow human beings on their own journeys through life. The psychological term for this is contact hypothesis; and, according to Harvard psychologist Gordon Allport, in ideal circumstances four conditions should be met for prejudice to actually become reduced through this method.[61]

Members from each group must have equal status.

Members from each group have common goals.

Members from each group work cooperatively.

Institutional support for the contact.

When thinking about the interactions our four Shire-hobbits have with outsiders, we should notice that all four conditions are in fact met on at least one occasion. In Rivendell, for example, though Elrond is the Lord of the Land, Frodo sits as an equal at his table; they all have the shared goal of destroying the Ring; they work together to come up with a plan to achieve this; and others, like Gandalf and Legolas, end up supporting the endeavor.

When thinking about our own interactions, we can learn to be extraordinary by applying the same strategies. But even if Allport's four conditions aren't always met, there is still evidence that having *some* mediated contact with those who lead different lives ends up

. . . .

61   Hopper, "What Is the Contact Hypothesis in Psychology?," sec. 2.

reducing prejudice. As Elizabeth Hopper notes, "The researchers found a larger effect on prejudice reduction when at least one of Allport's conditions was met. However, even in studies that didn't meet Allport's conditions, prejudice was still reduced—suggesting that Allport's conditions may improve relationships between groups, but they aren't strictly necessary."[62]

In situations like these, where Allport's conditions are not practical, so long as there is empathy from both parties, understanding and trust can be cultivated. Take, for instance, Frodo and Sam's meeting with Faramir in Ithilien. Here, there is not equal status—Frodo is at the mercy of Faramir and his soldiers—nor is there much institutional support to help mediate the relationship. But in the end, both grow in compassion for the other party. This is in large part due to each group listening to the other with empathy, putting aside their egos as they trust their intuition.

APPLYING THE WISDOM OF HOBBITS: NEW FOUND FELLOWSHIP

"The Company of the Ring shall be Nine; and the Nine Walkers shall be set against the Nine Riders that are evil. With you and your faithful servant, Gandalf will go; for this shall be his great task, and maybe the end of his labors."

"For the rest, they shall represent the other Free Peoples of the World: Elves, Dwarves, and Men. Legolas shall be for the Elves; and Gimli son of Glóin for the Dwarves. They are willing to go at least to the passes of the Mountains, and maybe beyond. For men you

. . . .

62   Ibid., sec. 3, para. 4.

shall have Aragorn son of Arathorn, for the Ring of Isildur concerns him closely."[63]

— Elrond of Rivendell

Like we did in the previous chapter, we end this one with a word about friendship. When we can step outside ourselves and learn to trust those whom we previously thought to be "outsiders," we can form new bonds and discover new forms of fellowship. What *The Lord of the Rings* teaches us is that when we do this, new opportunities for growth arise, propelling us toward extraordinary heights.

This is true for our four Hobbit companions, and it can also be true for us. The four Hobbits that left the Shire in September, TA 3018 are not the same four Hobbits that return over a year later. This is not just because they adventured through the Old Forest, the Barrow Downs, Moria, the Dead Marshes, the Emyn Muil, and Mordor; but because they learned to trust folks from all the different races of Middle-earth (some of them even going so far as settle down outside the borders of the Shire). For instance, after Merry and Pippin return from their journeys, while they mostly see the Shire as home (aiding Frodo and Sam in cleaning up Bag End after Lotho Sackville-Baggins and the ruffians have destroyed good portions of it prior to what is famously known as the Scouring of the Shire), they also take no issue with travelling back and forth between home and places like Minis Tirith and Edoras. In fact, both Merry and Pippin are buried in Gondor, laid to rest alongside King Elessar after his death at age 210. Their heroism becomes known far and wide, but they are also seen as heroes among their fellow Hobbits of the Shire (and Buckland!).

....

63   Tolkien, *The Fellowship of the Ring*, 309.

This is a lesson for all Hobbits, as well as all Big Folk; we grow when we step outside of our borders (literally for Merry and Pippin[64]). Whether we are Christians who befriend a group of Muslims, or whether we are straight white folks who befriend a gay Black couple, the takeaway is that we need to be in contact with those who may happen to lead very different lives from us. But more than that! When we encounter people unlike us, we need to lead with empathy and compassion. As my friend and author Derrick Day often says, these are the necessary basic ingredients for the cultivation of love.

All throughout *The Lord of the Rings*, love is championed. As the opening to Peter Jackson's film version of *The Fellowship of the Rings* professes, "Hobbits share a real love for things that grow."[65] This can be taken literally, of course; as we'll explore in the following chapter, Hobbits have a real love of gardening and farming. But it can also be taken more figuratively, as in, *there are Hobbits who love to grow as individuals*. Samwise Gamgee, for instance, is one of these. Prior to setting out with Frodo, he is unsure of himself, lacking any confidence whatsoever. As his love of Frodo increases, however, so does his tenacity and resolve, so much so that he will eventually become known as "Samwise the Brave"—perhaps the most courageous of acts being that he pursued and married Rosie Cotton, his true love, after his return to the Shire.

This brings us all the way back to something we explored throughout chapter 1—we need an adventure *and* a home. Too much adventuring

....

64   In *The Two Towers*, Merry and Pippen drink something known as Ent-draught, which was a drink made from river water and some unknown substances. It causes them to grow two to three inches, which is why at that point they would become the tallest Hobbits in history.

65   *The Fellowship of the Ring*, 09:56 to 09:59.

and we'll never set down any roots. As any seasoned gardener knows, this will stunt our growth and leave us susceptible to destruction. On the other hand, too much insulation from the outside world will leave us sheltered and small-minded, like the three gossiping Hobbits from The Ivy Bush. What is needed in life is balance, between an adventure and a home, between a quest to The Lonely Mountain or even Mordor, and a cozy hole in the ground at the end of Bagshot Row; a home where we can tend to our flower and vegetable gardens, smoke our pipe-weed, tell our tales over pints of ale, and enjoy the company of the very fine and extraordinary Hobbits, Elves, Dwarves, Men, and wizards we have in our own lives.

· 3 ·

tillers of the earth

*"The one small garden of a free gardener was all his need
and due, not a garden swollen to a realm; his own hands
to use, not the hands of others to command."*[66]

— FROM "THE TOWER OF CIRITH UNGOL"
IN *THE RETURN OF THE KING*

B alance has been one of the themes presented throughout the previous two chapters and it will be a theme of this one as well. But rather than talking about balancing our need for an adventure and a home, we will be exploring our need to live our lives in harmonious

66   Tolkien, *The Return of the King*, 186.

balance with the planet that bears our furry little Hobbit feet. To do that, we will again turn our attention to our halfling[67] friends for guidance, whose main passion for life—outside of drinking ales, smoking pipe-weed, and eating their second breakfasts—is, to quote Tolkien, "good tilled earth."[68]

THINGS THAT GROW

It's no secret that Hobbits love gardens. Perhaps the only thing they love more is the food that comes from them. From cabbage, carrots, tomatoes, and potatoes to herbs like sage and marjoram, they grow just about everything under the sun.[69] And even if there is no sun available, they'll still grow their favorite haunt—*mushrooms*. Aside from bacon, mushrooms are their passion. Combine the two in a well-seasoned skillet and you've got Hobbit-heaven. As Tolkien tells us, "Hobbits have a passion for mushrooms, surpassing even the greediest likings of Big People."[70]

Even when they are not busy getting their hands dirty in the soil, they are busy preparing the food and raw materials that come from it. They mill flour, process hops into ales and tobacco into pipe-weed, can vegetables for stews and jar jams for breads and cakes, and even

....

67 Halfling is a name for Hobbits originally used by the Dúnedain, and then by the Gondorians during the Third Age.

68 Tolkien, *The Fellowship of the Ring*, 1.

69 In Appendix B, I have provided a detailed list of all known plants, flowers, trees, and shrubs that grow in the Shire. There would no doubt be others; however, I have decided to include only those that are explicitly named by Tolkien himself.

70 Tolkien, *The Fellowship of the Ring*, 114.

make rope from a variety of natural sources (most likely hemp). But crops are not the only thing they "grow." Hobbits are, at a minimum, also familiar with pigs—Merry seemed to know what first-rate salted pork and rashers of bacon were[71]—and rabbits (or "conies," as Sam called them).

This passion for the earth is one thing that defines what it means to be a Hobbit. Just about everything is centered on this practice, and though they are not at all a God-fearing people, farming and gardening virtually serve as a de facto religion of sorts. In fact, unlike the clunkier and clumsier Big Folks, Hobbits have developed the almost magical skill of disappearing into the landscape swiftly and with ease, thanks in large part to their close friendship with the earth.[72]

Hobbits have such a strong relationship with the earth, in fact, that they often dig their homes into it. As we explored earlier, a good number of Hobbits live in holes in the ground (called smials), beautiful in their own right but unassuming and unpretentious above all else. Here, in the space between the earth and their own autonomy, is where Hobbits choose to live.

In a very strong sense, this relationship with the planet—full of all the ebbs and flows that come with it—is one thing that makes Hobbits quite unlike the other races of Middle-earth, especially Elves and Men. In Letter #197, Tolkien says the following of the Elven race and Men of Gondor:

> [Elves] wanted to have their cake and eat it: to live in the moral historical Middle-earth because they had become fond of it (and perhaps because they there had the advantages of a superior caste),

....

71   Tolkien, *The Two Towers*, 181.

72   Tolkien, *The Fellowship of the Ring*, 2.

and so tried to stop its change and history, stop its growth, keep it as a pleasaunce, even largely a desert, where they could be "artists"—and they were overburdened with sadness and nostalgic regret. In their way the Men of Gondor were similar: a withering people whose only "hallows" were their tombs.[73]

Hobbits, on the other hand, tend to live in the present moment in and alongside Middle-earth. They let it be what it is—full of change, full of seasons, full of the cycles of growth and decay—acting not as lords and ladies, but as tenders and stewards. This is one thing director Peter Jackson gets absolutely right in his films. The gardens adorned throughout Hobbiton and Bywater aren't depicted as sterile and too kempt, nor are they wild and overgrown; they are perfectly tended to without losing their "personality," as it were. In other words, the gardens of the Shire strike a perfect balance between tame and wild, between overgrown and over-pruned—not out of control but assuredly not prim and proper.

When musing about the Shire and its aesthetic, though the term is only thirty to forty years old, "permaculture" comes to mind. In this ecological philosophy, land management is done by observing what naturally flourishes, the focus being, not on individual crops, plants, or even gardens, but on "whole-system thinking," one that considers the entirety of the land being managed—from the plants themselves, to the pollinating bugs, soil pH, mulch quantity, and everything in between. This philosophy, as anyone who loves "good tilled earth" would attest, brings one into harmony with the land. *Does this not describe the average Hobbit?* English professor Lucas Niiler believes so, and asserts how Hobbits are, "caring farmers, green-thumbs," going

. . . .

73   Tolkien, *The Letters of J.R.R. Tolkien*, Letter #197.

on to add that, "beer-barley, rich tobacco, and beautiful flowers spring up out of their fields and gardens with just the gentle prod of a hoe."[74]

Anyone who has ever worked in a garden knows what a pleasure it is to work the ground with just a hoe. They also know the challenge of working the soil to such a place where only a hoe is needed. It takes time, effort, and buckets full of sweat. But once you are there, the earth no longer fights you. Instead, it works with you, like a seasoned dance partner who allows you to lead her all over the dance floor.

But this ecological philosophy is much more than simply creating a beautiful aesthetic. It is about caring for a planet that will become increasingly inhospitable if it is ignored and abused. As we will discover in the following section, should the peoples of Middle-earth turn their forests, rivers, meadows, and open plains into industrial hellscapes, they will quickly find themselves without a place to call their home. Applying such wisdom to us, then, have we not found that our Shire—our Arda—has started to become as desolate as the lands of Mordor? As the effects of climate change continue to worsen, and as more and more of our tropical rainforests are hewn, ironically in the name of progress, we know all too well this present danger, and, like Saruman, his Orcs, and, to only a slightly lesser degree, the Shire Hobbits all discovered, tragedy will find us unless we turn away from such evil.

. . . .

74   Niiler, "Green Reading," 276–85.

FROM PASTORAL PARADISE TO DESOLATE WASTELAND

A MIND OF METAL AND WHEELS

"He [Saruman] has a mind of metal and wheels; and he does not care for growing things, except as far as they serve him in the moment."[75]

— Gandalf

In direct contrast to the pastoral nature of the Shire is the industrialization of Isengard, first initiated by the wizard Saruman. Unlike Hobbits, who draw a sense of meaning from the land they cultivate by opting to live in harmony alongside it, Saruman sees the natural world as a resource to be plundered for the promotion of his industrial war machine. As Matthew Dickerson and Jonathan Evans put it, "Tolkien clearly associates Saruman with great harm to the environment and, more specifically, with technological progress that comes at the expense of life, nature, and the earth."[76]

Of course, in typical Tolkien fashion, he does not simply convey this information via a narrator. Instead, he is far more intentional than that. Much of what we hear about Saruman's abuses of power toward the ecology of Middle-earth comes directly from—and I would not be so hasty as to call him a tree—the most famous and oldest of all the Ents: Treebeard.

So, what is an Ent and why is it important that they are the ones who teach us about Tolkien's ecology?

. . . .

75 Tolkien, *The Two Towers*, 76.

76 Dickerson and Evans, *Ents, Elves, and Eriador*, 200.

In *The Silmarillion*, Yavanna (the Ainu[77]/Vala[78] responsible for everything that grows in Arda[79]) says that they are the Shepherds of the Trees, protecting the forests from all who wish to cause them harm.[80] Incidentally—though, again, please do *not* tell Treebeard this—their physical appearance resembles that of trees, which reflects their connection to the world in which they live. Professor of Literature Doron Darnov notices the following:

> Among the adjectives Tolkien uses, "fourteen foot high," "sturdy," "green and grey bark," "bushy," "twiggy," and "mossy," stand out and cultivate a sense of ecological materiality that highlights the connection between Ents and nature. Even more explicitly, instead of referring to Treebeard's "body," Tolkien uses the word "trunk" and therefore solidifies the idea that Ents are more akin to trees than to men, or for that matter, any of the other anthropomorphic races in Middle-earth.[81]

Again, all of this is intentional. As we witness in *The Two Towers*, when Saruman pushes too deeply into Fangorn Forest in search of even more resources, it is the Ents, led by Treebeard, who move to attack Isengard. To lay waste to the forest is to lay waste to an extension of the Ents; and to cut down an Ent is to cut down the forest. As Gandalf explains to Legolas, "Treebeard *is* Fangorn, the guardian of the forest

....

77 The Ainur, or Holy Ones, are the primordial spirits who existed with Ilúvatar, and with him created the Music of the Ainur.

78 The Valar are Ainur who entered Arda after its creation.

79 Arda is another term for the Earth, and encompasses both Middle-earth and Valinor, the place where many of the Elves live.

80 Tolkien, *The Silmarillion*, 41.

81 Darnov, "'A Mind of Metal and Wheels,'" sec. 1, para. 5.

(my emphasis)."[82] Driving the point home even more, here's Darnov once again:

> Ents give a voice to nature. The discursive and critical significance of this voice is clearly not lost on Tolkien or his Ents; it is with good reason that we learn about Saruman's industrialism through Treebeard: as Fangorn, Treebeard represents what our own forests and ecological victims would likely be telling us if they could speak for themselves.[83]

This is where the rubber meets the road. As human beings living in a post-industrialized world, we have two choices. On the one hand, we can live as Hobbits, where the lines between our own autonomy and the world in which we live blend. We can see ourselves as stewards of the earth—agrarian, pastoral, and rustic. If we have innovations or any semblance of industrialization, we are to be careful not to do anything that would cause harm to Arda. On the other hand, we can live as Saruman did, where nature is only there for us to conquer. When we take our walks through the forest (as Saruman once did[84]), we see the trees as natural resources that can fuel our lust for power and control. Our industrialization becomes only that which serves our needs.

What we choose depends upon us, but no matter the choice, consequences will follow. Treebeard and the Ents represent those consequences. For Saruman and the Orcs of Isengard, their choices eventually lead to their own personal devastation (though Saruman eventually *does* escape). They end up pushing too far into Fangorn Forest and the forest, albeit in their own time and never acting too hastily, push back, eventually laying waste to Orthanc and most who

. . . .

82   Tolkien *The Two Towers*, 107.

83   Darnov, "'A Mind of Metal and Wheels,'" sec. 1, para. 7.

84   Tolkien, *The Two Towers*, 75–76.

inhabited it (in what will come to be known as the Last March of the Ents).[85] The Hobbits, however, due to their love of Middle-earth and all things that grow on it, are destined for a different fate. As we will discuss in the following section, though many of them do in fact stumble, in the end they find their way back as caretakers of Arda by finding redemption, restoring what they let get away from them in their haste, ignorance, and desire for power.

THE RAZING AND SCOURING OF THE SHIRE

> "It was one of the saddest hours in their lives. The great chimney rose up before them; and as they drew near the old village across the Water, through rows of new mean houses along each side of the road, they saw the new mill in all its frowning and dirty ugliness: a great brick building straddling the stream, which it fouled with a steaming and stinking outflow. All along the Bywater Road every tree had been felled."[86]

As we have discussed throughout this chapter, Hobbits typically live in perfect communion with the earth. However, there are times when they do not quite live up to their reputation.[87]

. . . .

85 After the Ents destroy Saruman's dam, the river Isen floods the bowl of Isengard, submerging everything but Orthanc, killing many of the Orcs. Saruman lives, but he is confined to his tower. Eventually, however, he persuades the Ents to release him, and after they do, he leaves for the Shire where he lives out his final days as a hooligan in and around Hobbiton.

86 Tolkien, *The Return of the King*, 322.

87 Though we won't be exploring this in depth, there was a time when the Hobbits of Buckland and the trees of the Old Forest were at war. Sometime between T.A. 2340 and 3018, a group of trees attacked the hedge that divided Buckland from the Old Forest. In retaliation, the Hobbits burned hundreds of trees in a giant bonfire.

After the destruction of the Ring, for example, when Frodo, Sam, Merry, and Pippin return to the Shire, they find that it has been destroyed in many tragic ways: their Hobbit-holes are razed and replaced with Shirriff-houses and gates, the Old Mill is knocked down and replaced by a new mill, and their agrarian and pastoral hills are replaced by Saruman's industrialization, wrought with billowing smoke and the cacophonous clanging of gears, metal, and wheels. And yet, because of our extraordinary Hobbit friends, this is only the penultimate fate of the Shire, not its final one.

To save the Shire from even further ruin, Merry and Pippin, drawing on their experiences from the War of the Ring, join Farmer Cotton and others in leading a group of Hobbits in the Battle of Bywater. And though nineteen Hobbits give the ultimate sacrifice, they don't do so in vain, as the battle ends quickly, with approximately 100 ruffians being killed and the remaining Orcs and Men being driven out of the Shire.

Soon thereafter, Saruman and his henchman Wormtongue both suffer a similar fate. After yet again being verbally and physically abused by Saruman, Wormtongue finally snaps and cuts the wizard's throat. As he retreats down the lane, he is struck down by three Hobbit arrows and dies immediately, thus ending the final battle of the War of the Ring. The rest of the year is spent rebuilding homes, tunnels, and the Old Mill, and planting new trees where the old ones had been felled.

Fitting, isn't it, that Tolkien would pit two fates against each other in this way? On the one hand, you have the Hobbit ethic of being one with the land, which, prior to Saruman's invasion, leads to peace, prosperity, and happiness. On the other hand, you have the industrialized war machine that views the natural world as nothing more than an infinite resource, which eventually leads to tragedy, sadness, and a sobering loss of life. In the midst of both you have a race of people struggling to find their way, ultimately discovering redemption and restoration only after witnessing what would happen if they ever were to go astray and forget both who they are and their role in the world.

APPLYING THE WISDOM OF HOBBITS: FINDING BALANCE

"It is not our part to master all the tides of the world, but to do what is in us for the succour of those years wherein we are set, uprooting the evil in the fields that we know, so that those who live after may have clean earth to till. What weather they shall have is not ours to rule."[88]

— Gandalf

As we consider everything we have explored throughout this chapter, it would be easy to conclude that to spare ourselves from the ecological disasters that are inevitably coming our way—due to industrialization-induced climate change, deforestation, honeybee depopulation, and so on—all we need to do is start implementing universal policy change around the globe. Not that we shouldn't do that, but this alone would be too reductive a stance. As English Professor Lucas Niiler notes, "Tolkien's work makes the point that environmentalism, per se, cannot be grounded on simple actions or policy decisions. Rather, environmentalism comes about as a result of a change of thinking, a reassessment of human values."[89]

. . . .

88   Tolkien, *The Return of the King*, 160.

89   Niiler, Lucas P. "Timely, again: Tolkien's Fantastic Ecology," para. 14.

Our change of thinking, then, as Gandalf tells Aragorn, starts by focusing on what is right in front of us in the here and now, not those things that are entirely out of our control (like whether or not universal policy change ever happens). We are not to "master all the tides of the world;"[90] rather, we are to do what we can in our own little way. For most of us, kingship is not our lineage; so, for the Aragorns of the world, more could be done than, say, the Farmer Maggots or Farmer Cottons. But we all have our part to play. All that can be expected of each of us is to care for our little plots of land near the borders of our own Shire, defending them when threatened. Plus, as *The Lord of the Rings* so clearly teaches, it is not always the biggest and most powerful kings who are the most heroic; in fact, the reverse is often true.

And so, at the end of the day, what is needed is balance—balance between taking a "whole-systems approach" to the planet while also realizing that we are only one individual Hobbit who can only do so much. Sure, each decision we make for good or for ill can have huge consequences in our own personal lives and the lives of those around us. But to think we must save the world alone is too much of a burden to be placed on us. At the same time, we can also do our part in educating others so that they start to see the world through more ecologically-oriented eyes. This in turn will begin to move us incrementally forward toward a more universally sustainable model. Again, *balance*.

So, how do we do this in practical ways? Here are four Hobbit-inspired practices we can engage in in our own lives.

....

90   Tolkien, *The Return of the King*, 160.

PUTTING EVERYTHING INTO PRACTICE

First, we can plant a garden. Learn about what grows best in your climate and start planting those things. If you have long, hot summers, grow squash, tomatoes, peppers, melons, and blackberries. If you have cooler summers and live near the coast, you may be able to grow broccoli and leafy greens throughout the long summer months. Frost-free climates can accommodate these plants in the late fall and even in winter. The point being: find what is best for where you live and start getting your hands dirty.

Second, piggybacking off the first practice, we can learn as much as we can about permaculture and then start teaching others about it. As we learn and educate, we can also transform our own home environments so that the things we grow work in harmony with one another and the surrounding area. Find plants that bee populations love.[91] If you live in a region that suffers from frequent droughts, replace your lawn with drought-tolerant plants that you can put on a dripper system. Water is life, and if certain regions run out, it will be a disaster.

Third, we can stop using so much plastic. Replace those one-use water bottles with a metal canteen. Pick up some washable bags that you can reuse. Always make sure to recycle the plastic, aluminum, and glass that you use on a week-to-week basis.

Lastly, we can start supporting the politicians and companies who take an ecological approach and rejecting those who do not. If a company is run like Saruman ran his industrial war machine, refusing

....

91   For example, if blackberries grow in and around your property, instead of putting up a wood fence, you can vine them along a chain link fence. This will create a year-round green border that encourages bee activity. The more bees you have, the more pollination your fruit trees experience.

to do anything about the climate, then, if you are financially able, stop supporting them with your dollars until they change their ways of doing business. To encourage companies who couldn't care less about the planet is to encourage a fate similar to the one suffered by Isengard.

Of course, there is always more that can be done, but this should be a good start. Every single one of us can start living more like a Hobbit in this way, even those of us who live in urban areas. The rural, agrarian spirit, one firmly rooted in the earth, need not be exclusive to only those who live in the countryside. It's a frame of mind that can be applied in many ways and in different contexts. Just do what you can to promote Shire-living wherever you happen to find yourself, uprooting evil wherever you find it, so that those who come after us can have clean earth to till. What weather they have is not ours to determine[92] (though if we can somehow reverse climate change, maybe they will have some decent weather, too).

. . . .

92   Tolkien, *The Return of the King*, 160.

PART II

....

hobbit will

A free will, perchance?
Better yet, a freed will, perhaps.

· 4 ·
great power in small packages

"'No!' cried Gandalf, springing to his feet. 'With that power I should have power too great and terrible. And over me the Ring would gain a power still greater and more deadly.' His eyes flashed and his face was lit as by a fire within. 'Do not tempt me! For I do not wish to become like the Dark Lord himself. Yet the way of the Ring to my heart is by pity, pity for weakness and the desire of strength to do good. Do no tempt me! I dare not take it, not even to keep it safe, unused. The wish to wield it would be too great for my strength. I shall have such need of it. Great perils lie before me.'"[93]

— FROM "THE SHADOW OF THE PAST," IN
THE FELLOWSHIP OF THE RING

93   Tolkien, *The Fellowship of the Ring*, 67–68.

E ven though we have been exploring the tales of some of the more extraordinary Hobbits in history, as a people they are not traditionally regarded as great heroes. Compared to Men and Elves, little is even known of their history. Though the Elves, being great historians, indeed kept records dating back to the Elder Days, whereby Hobbits trace their lineage, nothing is mentioned of them in the Elves' vast array of records. And yet, as Tolkien says in the Prologue to *The Fellowship of the Ring*, "It is clear that Hobbits had, in fact, lived quietly in Middle-earth for many long years before other folk became even aware of them."[94]

Of course, Hobbit modesty should not be too much of a surprise for us. As we've already discussed at length, Hobbits—especially those who live in and around the Shire—are a quiet and humble people, oftentimes to a fault. They can be sheltered, private, and skeptical, sometimes almost xenophobic. But even those who are not so close-minded are still quite unassuming and "boring" (in the best way possible). Rather than heroic adventures involving run-ins with dragons, Orcs, and Black Riders, they typically enjoy growing food, smoking pipe-weed, preparing food, drinking ales, eating food, throwing parties, and, if the mood strikes them, eating more food. Journeying on great adventures is for the Big Folk; tending to a garden or milling flour is for the Little Folk. This is why the stories of Meriadoc Brandybuck, Peregrin Took, Samwise Gamgee, Frodo Baggins, and Bilbo Baggins bring us such unexpected and astonishing heroes.

. . . .

94   Ibid., 3.

THE HERO'S JOURNEY[95]

Before we explore the unique heroism of Hobbits, we should first discuss the concept of the hero's journey.

The hero's journey goes by many names—the monomyth, the ultimate narrative archetype, the mythological archetype—but it is essentially a way of describing the journey one takes when going on an adventure. Put most simply, it is a story template, illustrated most clearly in the following way:

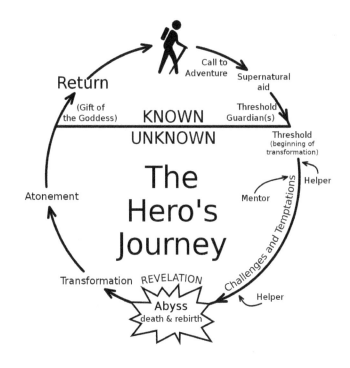

. . . .

95 The following section has been modified from something I used in an essay for the yet to be released book *Beauty in Ordinary Things*, edited by Yvette Cantu-Schneider.

While there have been psychologists, sociologists, and other scholars who have proposed similar story templates, it was professor of literature Joseph Campbell who first brought these ideas and concepts into the public sphere. Influenced by Carl Jung's analytical psychology, Campbell initially describes the narrative pattern in *The Hero with a Thousand Faces* as follows:

> A hero ventures forth from the world of common day into a region of supernatural wonder: fabulous forces are there encountered and a decisive victory is won: the hero comes back from this mysterious adventure with the power to bestow boons on his fellow man.[96]

Of course, the hero's journey is but a template, so not all stories follow the same *exact* pattern. Like we discussed in the previous chapter, the supernatural (i.e., any religion outside of a direct relationship with Arda) is not something Hobbits care too much about. However, while there is no explicit mention of God by Hobbit writers, supernatural forces do in fact impress themselves upon our halfling friends despite them not having language for it. As we will discuss in later chapters, forces outside of the characters move their arcs forward toward their eventual culmination of atonement and return.

THE THREE "ACTS"

While Campbell describes seventeen stages of the monomyth in *The Hero with A Thousand Faces*, we will distill these down into three "acts." They are as follows:
- Departure/Separation
- Initiation/Descent
- Return

....

96   Campbell, *The Hero with a Thousand Faces*, 23.

DEPARTURE

Before a hero's departure, they live a "normal" life. Perhaps they tend to a garden at the end of Bagshot Row or tend bar evenings at The Green Dragon Inn. Life then throws them a curveball. For Bilbo, it comes in the way of thirteen Dwarves and one wizard showing up at his stoop. For Frodo, it is being gifted a magic ring that upends his cozy life. For Sam, it is being caught by Gandalf for eavesdropping on Bag End after the shenanigans that take place during and after Bilbo's birthday party. But no matter what the cause, for any person (or Hobbit) to take this journey, one needs to first depart from their normal life. Only after that can they embrace the adventure ahead.

INITIATION

The initiation "act" is where the character gets to the point of no return. They traverse a threshold, so to speak. At this threshold is where our heroes face trials and tribulations, sometimes completely alone, but more often with the help of an aide.

Thinking about Frodo and Sam's story; when Frodo is given the One Ring by his uncle Bilbo, they both end up crossing a threshold from which they cannot return. Though Frodo tries, and fails—by offering the Ring to Gandalf (who wisely declines)—what had been done could never be undone.

Eventually, our hero will reach what Campbell calls "the innermost cave," or the chief crisis of their story arc. For Frodo and Sam, there are many of these *literal* crises where they nearly die at the hands of some wicked monster: Frodo's capture by the Barrow-wight, his stabbing at the hands of the Witch King, his run-in with Shelob and subsequent imprisonment by Shagrat's Orc party near Cirith Ungol. There are also the more abstract crises both Frodo and Sam face, as in the Ring's perpetual and unrelenting pull to be placed on their fingers.[97] No matter which arc we are exploring, at some point in the story, things will come to a head and our heroes will have to overcome their main obstacle.

RETURN

After the main enemy or obstacle is defeated and overcome, our heroes will reenter "normal" life, albeit drastically changed. They will possess a wisdom they never had prior to their adventure, often imparting it onto others as an act of kindness and generosity. Thinking again about Frodo and Sam's story, after they return from Mordor and help defeat Saruman and the ruffians who razed the Shire, they live the next part of their lives as changed Hobbits. Yes, Frodo carries wounds with him that will not heal until he travels West to the Undying Lands, but before leaving the Shire for the final time, he imparts the wisdom he has gained to his friends and countrymen as best as he's able. The same exact thing could be said of Sam—from henceforth affectionally known as Samwise the Brave—though because he was never harmed in the same way as Frodo, the Shire will again become his home for decades to come.

Thinking first about Frodo: there are three distinct things he does to better the Shire after his return. First, as acting Deputy Mayor, he gets rid of all the Shirriffs except for those who are needed to maintain order in the Shire. Thus, he undoes what had been done by Lotho,

. . . .

97   While Sam only held the Ring for a short time, he is still considered one of the Ring-bearers. And as such, he too was tempted in the same way as Frodo (though obviously for Sam to a much lesser degree). For instance, after Shelob attacks Frodo, Sam, believing Frodo was now dead, takes the Ring with the intention to complete the final portion of the quest on his own. As he holds it, the Ring tempts him with perhaps the one thing he desires more than anything, visions of a giant garden all for himself.

MATTHEW J. DISTEFANO

Saruman, and the ruffians.[98] Second, Frodo aids Sam in offering him much needed advice about whether to marry Rosie Cotton: "You want to get married, and yet you want to live with me in Bag End too? But my dear Sam, how easy! Get married as soon as you can, and then move in with Rosie. There's room enough in Bag End for as big a family as you could wish for."[99] Lastly, after having their first child, Sam and Rosie aren't sure what to name her, so Frodo comes up with the perfect solution: "Well, Sam, what about *elanor*, the sun-star, you remember the little golden flower in the grass of Lothlórien?"[100] All of these acts are carried out because of what Frodo has learned from his journeys, the confidence he's gained from them, as well as how close he and Sam have become as a result of their shared experiences.

For Sam, it is simple: give himself to the service of his beloved Shire by doing three things, 1) planting saplings in all the places the most beautiful and treasured trees had been destroyed, 2) serving as Mayor of the Shire for seven consecutive seven-year terms, and 3) marrying Rosie Cotton and having thirteen children: Elanor the Fair, Frodo, Rose, Merry, Pippin, Goldilocks, Hamfast, Daisy, Primrose, Bilbo, Ruby, Robin, and Tolman. Like Frodo, had Sam (who was initially nothing more than a reluctant and shy Hobbit only dreaming of Elves, mountains, and Dwarven cities) not journeyed on his adventure to Mordor and back, he would not have had the courage to be able to do any of these things.

....

98   Tolkien, *The Return of the King*, 329.

99   Ibid., 332.

100 Ibid., 334.

95

HEROISM IN MANY FORMS

"There is a lot more in Bilbo than you guess, and a deal more than he has any idea of himself."[101]

— Gandalf

Without a doubt, when we reflect on the heroism found in *The Hobbit* or *The Lord of the Rings*, it's easy to first think about Hobbits. After all, they are the main characters of both tales. But when we zoom back and take a 30,000-foot view—perhaps sitting atop the Great Eagles of Manwë—and look at the entire Legendarium of Middle-earth, their heroism becomes more of a surprise. Hobbits, if you will remember, are of little consequence in the grand scheme of things. And that's precisely what makes *these* tales—*The Hobbit* and *The Lord of the Rings*—so extraordinary.

What would be more expected is that Men, Elves, or even Dwarves would become the main heroes. To some degree, they are. Aragorn, the eventual King of Gondor, for instance, follows the path of the hero. His normal life is that as Strider, a Ranger of the North, but his transformed life, after facing many trials and tribulations, is as respected King. Gandalf, everyone's favorite snarky wizard, has a similar trajectory that is even visually represented by his transformation from Grey to White. And Boromir, brief as his journey is in comparison to the other members of the Fellowship, even undergoes a transformation after attempting to steal the Ring from Frodo.

We could continue by mentioning Legolas and Gimli, Galadriel, Théoden, Faramir, and others, but the point here is that the heroes of Middle-earth all follow a similar path. However, all are unique in

. . . .

101 Tolkien, *The Hobbit*, 19.

their own ways. Some rise to hero status by exerting power, others by showing great restraint, but all do so by showing bravery and courage in the face of perilous circumstances, most of which are brought on by the One Ring.

RESISTING THE DESIRE FOR POWER

One crucial factor in our heroes' stories is they will all, at some point, have to wrestle with the desire to grasp the Ring. Most fail; only a few succeed. But all are changed in some way because of their interaction with it.

Frodo, as we know, is perhaps the most impacted by it. For him, it is a life-draining burden that increases the longer he carries it. The same could be said of Bilbo's ownership of the Ring; however, because he isn't under the same stress from Sauron's forces as Frodo, it affects Bilbo a bit less (though it does stretch him thin, like butter scraped over too much bread).[102] Sméagol, however, is a different story altogether. From the moment the "former" Hobbit grasps it, to the day he falls into the Cracks of Mt. Doom, the Ring controls his mind.

The Ring does not just impact those who carry it. Both Boromir and Aragorn, for example, are tempted by its power, with only Aragorn able to resist its hold on him. Later in the journey, Boromir's brother Faramir is able to do something his brother couldn't—resist the urge to take the Ring from Frodo. As the quote to open this chapter shows us, Gandalf too has to resist any urge to take it from Frodo (even though it is freely offered to him). And Galadriel, whilst the Company is in Lothlórien, also resists the Ring, realizing that darkness will overtake her should she obtain it.

. . . .

102   Tolkien, *The Fellowship of the Ring*, 34.

All this leads me to one conclusion: Hobbits like Frodo, Sam, and Bilbo truly are heroic. They are able to possess the Ring without having it completely consume them. Sure, as we will discuss in the following chapter, Frodo is not actually able to part with it upon arriving at Mt. Doom. However, he has borne it over hundreds and hundreds of miles without completely losing his identity as a true and noble Hobbit. This is no small feat, and he should be recognized for it.

Should any from the race of Men, Elves, or wizards have gotten their hands on it, who knows what would have happened? Nothing good, I'd imagine. As Gandalf readily admits, "With that power I should have power too great and terrible. And over me the Ring would gain a power still greater and more deadly [...] Do not tempt me! For I do not wish to become like the Dark Lord himself."[103]

It takes a lot of wisdom to show such restraint—wisdom not everyone in Gandalf's position possesses. Saruman, for instance, shows no such restraint when he finds out about the Ring. He only speaks of wisdom. In reality, it is mere foolishness veiled in language about power, order, and rule:

> "We must have power, power to order all things as we will, for that good which only the Wise can see."

> "And listen, Gandalf, my old friend and helper!" he said, coming near and speaking now in a softer voice. "I said we, for we it may be, if you will join with me. A new Power is rising. Against it the old allies and policies will not avail us at all. There is no hope left in Elves or dying Númenor. This then is one choice before you, before us. We may join with that Power. It would be wise, Gandalf. There is hope that way. Its victory is at hand; and there will be rich reward for those that aided it. As the Power grows, its proved friends will also grow; and the Wise, such as you and I, may with patience

come at last to direct its courses, to control it. We can bide our time, we can keep our thoughts in our hearts, deploring maybe evils done by the way, but approving the high and ultimate purpose: Knowledge, Rule, Order; all the things that we have so far striven in vain to accomplish, hindered rather than helped by our weak or idle friends. There need not be, there would not be, any real change in our designs, only in our means."[104]

But Gandalf knows better. He knows that to give in to the Ring's power is to never be able to come back to one's former, truest self. Saruman's folly, among other things, is that he believes he can join with the power of the Ring and of Sauron and continue to maintain his own will and agency. Gandalf knows this is imprudent, however, and immediately but appropriately calls Saruman "foolish."[105]

And he is absolutely right; it is foolish to ever think one could master the power of the Ring. Everyone who comes into contact with it is impacted in some way, almost always negatively (save for Tom Bombadil, but that's a topic for another time). Sam is tempted by its power. Bilbo, as we recently stated, becomes stretched thin, like butter scraped over too much bread.[106] Frodo is so burdened by the Ring that he has to leave the Shire for good, even after its destruction. Sméagol becomes so gone that any semblance of his former self has been lost forever. Boromir attempts to sabotage the Fellowship by stealing it from Frodo. Only Faramir and Aragorn are able to resist the Ring, but only by not grasping at it or even touching it.

This is why everyone just mentioned, as well as those not (Legolas, Gimli, Merry, and Pippin), are heroes in their own right. Though

....

104   Ibid., 291.

105   Ibid.

106   Ibid., 34.

such a title is problematic, as we'll soon discover in the next chapter, the title of "hero" is the most fitting in light of what we know about the journey they must take.

APPLYING THE WISDOM OF HOBBITS: FRIENDSHIP AND HEROISM

There are many heroes who live in Middle-earth before and during the War of the Ring—great men and women of power and prestige, noble Elves and fearless Dwarves, wise wizards. But some of the greatest heroes of all stand no higher than four feet. They are not clad in thick armor, nor do they wield a sword like Andúril.[107] Instead, they wear green and yellow tunics and display the greatest power of all: the restraint to say *no* to the power of the Ring.

Many of us will have to resist power throughout our lives. Power and our desire for it will come to us in many forms, just like it does with the Ring. Not for nothing, but when Sam is tempted by the Ring after Frodo's imprisonment near Cirith Ungol, it is an invitation that tugs at his personal heartstrings—a huge garden all to himself. We will face these same temptations for power, innocuous enough on the surface, but devastating should we succumb to the greed from which they stem. Whether it's the sense of power we get from lording over others at work, or from forcing our children to do what we want them to do when we want them to do it, or from any number of other common life situations we will face in life, all should be resisted in the same way Hobbits resist the Ring of Power. To succumb to

. . . .

107 Andúril is the name of the sword passed down
through Elendil, eventually to Aragorn.

any of power's attempts to sway us is to ensure a life of tragedy and suffering. Sméagol finds this out the hard way. So too does Saruman, Wormtongue, and even Sauron himself. The only way to avoid such a fate is to be like Frodo and Sam. Reject power as long as you're able and hope that in doing so you have a Shire to which you may return.

This struggle against the temptation for power again leads us to the importance of friendship and fellowship. None of our heroes can resist the Ring without having love in their hearts for one another; while those who fail to resist its power have little (or even none at all). Love is the greatest difference in all of this; indeed, it is the greatest difference between an enslaved Sméagol and a hero like Frodo.

Prior to taking responsibility for the Ring, Frodo is pure in heart. He wants what is best for the Shire, for others. Like almost all Hobbits, he loves good tilled earth. He loves the trees and the starry skies above them. He loves flowers and gardens and all things that grow. Sméagol on the other hand already has malice in his heart. When his cousin Déagol finds the Ring, Sméagol is already a Hobbit who is at best indifferent about all these things, about a love of trees, starry skies, flowers that bloom in spring. As Gandalf tells Frodo in "The Shadow of the Past:"

> The most inquisitive and curious-minded of that family was called Sméagol. He was interested in roots and beginnings; he dived into deep pools; he burrowed under trees and growing plants; he tunneled into green mounds; and he ceased to look up at the hilltops, or the leaves on trees, or the flowers opening in the air: his head and his eyes were downward.[108]

....

108 Tolkien, *The Fellowship of the Ring*, 57.

After the Ring's discovery, Sméagol immediately turns on Déagol and murders him. Without so much as a second thought, he turns to violence. This only proves that without a foundation built on love for others, the Ring will further corrupt the already corrupted.

So, it is for us as well! If we don't have true friendship and fellowship, our desire for power will too often get the best of us, just as it did for Sméagol. But if we remain true to the Hobbit spirit of loving the earth and every creature who walks upon it, swims in it, and soars above it, then we will be able to resist its pull toward darkness, leaning on those around us whom we love, cherish, and adore.

·· 5 ··

the messiness of heroism

"'Deserves it! I daresay he does. Many that live deserve death. And some that die deserve life. Can you give it to them? Then do not be too eager to deal out death in judgement. For even the very wise cannot see all ends. I have not much hope that Gollum can be cured before he dies, but there is a chance of it. And he is bound up with the fate of the Ring. My heart tells me that he has some part to play yet, for good or ill, before the end; and when that comes, the pity of Bilbo may rule the fate of many—yours not least.'"[109]

— GANDALF, FROM "THE SHADOW OF THE PAST," IN *THE FELLOWSHIP OF THE RING*

. . . .

109 Tolkien, *The Fellowship of the Ring*, 65–66.

In the previous chapter, we explored some of the ways in which heroism shows up in the Third Age of Middle-earth, focusing primarily on the subtle qualities Hobbits possess—restraint, self-control, and willpower. In this chapter, we are going to complicate matters a bit by exploring all the ways in which separating heroes from villains, good guys from bad guys, is not a cut-and-dried thing. We will examine how Tolkien does a masterful job at blurring the lines between the categories we typically use to describe our favorite characters.

Of course, the recognition of ambiguity is not to say there aren't out-and-out villains in Tolkien's Legendarium, or those who aren't heroes through and through; it just means that sometimes our heroes are messy and our villains complicated. As Tolkien scholar Dr. Amy Amendt-Raduege writes:

> Nobody starts out as a hero in Tolkien's stories, not even the heroes themselves. They have to grow into their roles. Furthermore, different characters reach their heroic peak at different points in the story, during different events and in different places. The result is a sort of ebb and flow of heroism, where some characters reach their finest achievement fairly early on in the story, and others don't reach their full potential until the very last chapters.[110]

In the section that follows, we are going to discuss just a handful of these characters, digging deeper into the inner workings of some of the more famous (or infamous) of all the Hobbits.

....

110   Amendt-Raduege, "A Seed of Courage," 4–5.

COMPLICATED CHARACTERS

FRODO AND THE RING

> "'I have come,' he said. 'But I do not choose now to do what I came to do. I will not do this deed. The Ring is mine!' And suddenly, as he set it on his finger, he vanished from Sam's sight."[111]

— Frodo Baggins

For all the praise Frodo deserves for his role in the Ring's destruction, it shouldn't be lost on us that, in the end, he is unable to throw it into the fires of Mt. Doom. Upon the precipice he stands, having travelled nearly 1,800 treacherous miles,[112] and he just can't bring himself to do it. Why? There are two explanations: 1) the Ring's power over Frodo has become *that* domineering,[113] or 2) there is some weakness inside Frodo that he thinks could be filled by the Ring.[114] Either way, Frodo has burdensomely carried the Ring for 185 days, and in that time, it has become too much to bear. As Tolkien explains in Letter #246, "At the last moment the pressure of the Ring would reach its maximum— impossible, I should have said, for any one to resist, certainly after long possession, months of increased torment, and when starved and exhausted."[115]

. . . .

111 Tolkien, *The Return of the King*, 239.

112 http://lotrproject.com/timedistance/.

113 This is the Manichean view: the philosophy that states how the forces of good and evil are in opposition with one another.

114 This is the Boethian view: the philosophy that states how evil is simply the privation of good.

115 Tolkien, *The Letters of J.R.R. Tolkien*, Letter #246.

Should this surprise us? No, not really. It is foreshadowed near the beginning of *The Fellowship of the Ring*, when Gandalf challenges Frodo to throw it into the fireplace at Bag End. Just minutes after learning about it, Frodo is already beholden to its power.

> Frodo drew the Ring out of his pocket again and looked at it. It now appeared plain and smooth, without mark or device that he could see. The gold looked very fair and pure, and Frodo thought how rich and beautiful was its colour, how perfect was its roundness. It was an admirable thing and altogether precious. When he took it out he had intended to fling it from him into the very hottest part of the fire. But he found now that he could not do so, not without a great struggle. He weighed the Ring in his hand, hesitating, and forcing himself to remember all that Gandalf had told him; and then with an effort of will he made a movement, as if to cast it away—but he found that he had put it back in his pocket.[116]

That is not to say the events of the rest of the books are foreordained or that Frodo has no will of his own—we will talk more about that in the following chapter—but it does mean that the Ring needs very little time to corrupt even the most noble of Hobbits.

Of course, most authors would have given us a quite different and contradictory final Mt. Doom scene. For most, no matter what, Frodo—*our* hero—would have prevailed. Even if he puts the Ring on and at some point, decides not to destroy it, that "still small voice" would have eventually triumphed. But not here, not for Tolkien. Instead, in Middle-earth, evil seems to destroy itself. It is not overcome by the power of good; it literally works against itself, leading to its own collapse. By drawing the Ring to himself, Sauron draws it right into the only fires that could destroy it. Notice that none of our

. . . .

116 Tolkien, *The Fellowship of the Ring*, 67–68.

"good" characters actually destroy anything in the end; the evil of the world is destroyed by itself—the Ring falls into the Cracks and thus the Tower falls to the ground.

If we can say *anything* about Frodo's contribution to the end of evil, it is that through his pity, Sauron is vanquished. Both Frodo *and* Bilbo's pity, really—as well as Sam's. All three Hobbits have their chance to kill Gollum—Bilbo when he first meets him deep in the heart of the Misty Mountains, and Frodo and Sam on numerous occasions throughout their shared journeys—and yet all three choose to stay their hands. Had either done the opposite, reasonably opting instead to kill the sneaking, lurking trickster, then would the world have been saved? Perhaps. Ilúvatar would likely have found some way to continue to work towards a redeemed and reconciled end, but not in the same manner, not in the same way. Bilbo, Frodo, and Sam's pity make it possible for Gollum to "interfere" with Frodo at the Cracks of Mt. Doom, which in turn leads to both Gollum and the Ring being destroyed. Here's how Professor David Waito explains it:

> Providentially, Frodo and Sam are rewarded for their compassion when Gollum inadvertently saves the Ring Quest. Gollum's final act, i.e., biting off the Ring and Frodo's finger and falling into the fire, is ironically both a betrayal and a service to Frodo. Gollum's intentions were not benign, and he cannot be acclaimed as the savior of the Ring Quest. The true saviors are pity and forgiveness. Without these, the quest was doomed to fail. Tolkien's message is that these benevolent virtues which enable the destruction of the Ring of Power are the same virtues the [sic] provide protection from greed, excessive pride, and uncontrollable lust for power.[117]

. . . .

117 Waito, "The Shire Quest," 169.

This, however, does not mean *Frodo* fails at what he sets out to do. He bears the Ring farther and for longer than anyone else, and delivers it to the place where it can end up destroying itself. As Tolkien explains in Letter #192:

> Frodo deserved all honour because he spent every drop of his power of will and body, and that was just sufficient to bring him to the destined point, and no further. Few others, possibly no others of his time, would have got so far.[118]

However, like all of Middle-earth's characters, Frodo is complex. It cannot be lost on us that though Tolkien is completely correct, Frodo, like Isildur before him, indeed succumbs to the power of evil, but not because he is evil himself; it's simply because of just how deceptive the Ring's power can be. Incidentally, this self-reflective ability actually helps inspire a more empathetic and merciful Frodo, who in the end realizes that without someone like Gollum, the Ring can never be destroyed: "Do you remember Gandalf's words: *Even Gollum may have something yet to do?* But for him, Sam, I could not have destroyed the Ring. The Quest would have been in vain, even at the bitter end."[119]

POOR, POOR SMÉAGOL

> "Bilbo almost stopped breathing, and went stiff himself. He was desperate. He must get away, out of this horrible darkness, while he had any strength left. He must fight. He must stab the foul thing, put its eyes out. It meant to kill him. No, not a fair fight. He was invisible now. Gollum had no sword. Gollum had not actually

....

118 Tolkien, *The Letters of J.R.R. Tolkien*, Letter #192.

119 Tolkien, *The Return of the King*, 241.

threatened to kill him, or tried yet. And he was miserable, alone, lost. A sudden understanding, a pity mixed with horror, welled up in Bilbo's heart: a glimpse of endless unmarked days without light or hope of betterment, hard stone, cold fish, sneaking and whispering. All these thoughts passed in a flash of a second. He trembled. And then quite suddenly in another flash, as if lifted by a new strength and resolve, he leaped [...] straight over Gollum's head he jumped."[120]

Like Frodo, Sméagol knows the power of the Ring. Intimately. However, unlike Frodo, it quickly consumes his mind and drives him to the darkest places one can possibly go—both literally and figuratively. Literally, the Ring drives him deep under the Misty Mountains, where he will be sheltered from the sun, trees, flowers, and cool breezes for hundreds of years, only to come out from hiding on rare occasions. During this time, the Ring also stretches Sméagol's heart and mind thinner and thinner, until he can no longer recognize the Hobbit he once was. This is how Gollum is born.

Again though, it would be too reductive to think of Gollum as simply "the bad guy." Yes, he is mischievous beyond comprehension. He is to never be trusted, as his mind is set upon only one thing: obtaining the Ring. He will do anything to get his bony little hands on it, including killing his own best friend. However—and this is one of the things some people don't like about Tolkien's characters, but what also makes them so intriguing, timeless, and true to form—there are two things we must remember: 1) that Gollum is never wholly

. . . .

120 Tolkien, *The Hobbit*, 86–87.

ruined by the Ring,[121] and 2) if Frodo (or any number of Hobbits we have all grown to love) had been given more time, he too could have easily become just like Gollum. In fact, Gandalf alludes to such a possibility: "'I think it is a sad story,' said the wizard, 'and it might have happened to others, even to some hobbits that I have known.'"[122]

Imagine, if you will, the scene at the Cracks of Doom. But instead of Gollum showing up, he never comes. Maybe he gets arrested by some soldiers of Gondor or captured by a group of Orcs. Or, perhaps Sam or Frodo had killed him while in Ithilien. Either way, he isn't there. Sam, thinking that Frodo is going to throw the Ring into the fires below, lets down his guard. Then Frodo does the unthinkable— he refuses, slipping on the Ring, thus also slipping out of sight—and walks down the mountainside.

Now, ask yourself this: what would have become of Frodo if Gollum never shows up? Would the same thing that happened to Sméagol not have eventually happened to our main character? We can only speculate, but it seems reasonable to believe that Frodo may have eventually ended up in exactly the same predicament: beholden to the Ring and its deceptive power, stretched thinner and thinner, "like butter scraped over too much bread," as his uncle Bilbo once put it.[123]

This is why Frodo pities Gollum. He knows deep down Gollum was once a Hobbit—a Stoorish Hobbit, in fact, living in and around

. . . .

121 To quote Gandalf: "Deserves it! I daresay he does. Many that live deserve death. And some that die deserve life. Can you give it to them? Then do not be too eager to deal out death in judgement. For even the very wise cannot see all ends. I have no much hope that Gollum can be cured before he dies, but there is a chance of it (Tolkien, *The Fellowship of the Ring*, 65).

122 Tolkien, *The Fellowship of the Ring*, 59.

123 Ibid., 34.

the Gladden Fields. And as such, Frodo recognizes himself in Gollum. He recognizes what he could become should he fail in his mission to destroy the Ring.

SAMWISE THE BRAVE

> "Sam came on. He was reeling like a drunken man, but he came on. And Shelob cowed at last, shrunken in defeat, jerked and quivered as she tried to hasten from him. She reached the hole, and squeezed down, leaving a trail of green-yellow slime, she slipped in, even as Sam hewed a last stroke at her dragging legs. Then he fell to the ground."[124]

Perhaps the most endearing character in all Middle-earth is Samwise Gamgee. A gardener by trade, Sam is as simple and basic as any Hobbit. Except deep down, he's not. Inside, he desires to be brave and adventurous; he just doubts himself too much to take that step onto the Road.[125] That is, until he stumbles upon Frodo and Gandalf's initial conversation about the Ring, and as they say, the rest is history.

What makes Sam so remarkable is that while there is no great warrior lineage in his family, no name recognition, he steps into history and makes a name for himself. First, he does this the minute he takes up the task to join Frodo on his adventure out of the Shire. He does it again in Buckland before heading off through the Old Forest. Then, he does it at Amon Hen, when Frodo tries to give him and everyone else the slip. Not even knowing how to swim, Sam runs headlong into the Anduin River and nearly drowns. As the pair draw closer and closer to Mordor, Sam proves his mettle and bravery

....

124 Tolkien, *The Two Towers*, 383–84.

125 Tolkien, *The Fellowship of the Ring*, 82.

THE WISDOM OF HOBBITS

over and over again—fighting with Gollum on numerous occasions, running into the tower at Cirith Ungol in search of Frodo, defeating Shelob after she had incapacitated Frodo, and even putting the Ring on and then willingly giving it back after realizing Frodo had not been killed by the giant spider.

If you were to try and tell the Sam who hadn't yet left the Shire any of the feats he would accomplish, he'd probably think you had been drinking too much Old Winyards. He is a bashful and ordinary Hobbit with a sort of "ah shucks" personality. I imagine him blushing any time attention is paid to him. But the post-Mordor Sam is a different character all together. From replanting all the trees that were cut down in the razing of the Shire, to serving as Mayor of Michel Delving for seven consecutive seven-year terms, to marrying Rosie Cotton and having thirteen children with her, Sam becomes the epitome of a confident and extraordinary Hobbit. And yet, he never loses that charm he started out with. He never becomes overconfident or brash; just a shy confident—probably walking around Hobbiton with his shoulders back a little farther and his chest out a little more.

Moreover, Sam never sees himself as a hero, just "the servant of a great master," as Dr. Amendt-Raduege puts it.[126] But that's exactly what he is—or, rather, *becomes*. And while this heroic development is present in all of Tolkien's characters—as Amendt-Raduege argues—it is seen in no place greater than Sam.

MERRY & PIPPIN

"'I wish Merry was here,' he heard himself saying, and quick thoughts raced through his mind, even as he watched the enemy come

. . . .

126   Amendt-Raduege, "A Seed of Courage," 5.

charging to the assault. 'Well, well, now at any rate I understand poor Denethor a little better. We might die together, Merry and I, and since we must die, why not? Well, as he is not here, I hope he'll find an easier end. But now I must do my best.'"[127]

Both Meriadoc Brandybuck and Peregrin Took are like those friends everyone from your small, humble hometown knows, who then go onto discover plutonium or start the next Google or Microsoft. That is to say, they were both Shire-famous early on but then become famous-famous.

As we briefly mentioned in the introduction, the Brandybuck family began as the Oldbuck clan, who were Thains of the Shire for ten generations in a row before moving to Buckland over the Brandywine River. The Tooks, as we've discussed numerous times, were known for their adventurous spirit as it seemed to run through their veins. Not for nothing, but to have something "Tookish" rise up in you is to swell with bravery and courage, as someone does prior to setting out on a dangerous adventure.

So, numbering Hobbits like Merry and Pippin among the heroic should not be too much of a surprise. What may surprise perhaps the more casual fan among us is the fact that Merry and Pippin are *very different* characters. Sure, we see them as *the* dynamic duo of Middle-earth—a close second is Gimli and Legolas—and while there is some truth to that, they are each quite unique. Merry, for instance, is responsible. He knows about the Ring long before he says anything; he organizes the conspiracy to get Frodo out of the Shire; and he finds out the Nazgûl are in Bree at the same time the Hobbits

. . . .

127 Tolkien, *The Return of the King*, 176.

are.[128] Pippin, on the other hand, is curious and rather aloof. While the other companions have a cautious seriousness about them—how could you not if unknown Black Riders are after you? Pippin is busy cracking jokes and earning the nickname Gandalf would famously give him: fool of a Took!

Again, however, we are talking about Tolkien's characters, and so they are far more complex and complicated than my brief and might I admit reductive summaries acknowledge. Merry is not just serious and planful, he is also casual and playful, as we find out after their defeat of Saruman at Orthanc. And Pippin is not just some foolish jester; he shows immense grief and despair after thinking his best friend has died in the Battle of the Pelennor Fields. Dr. Amy Amendt-Raduege notices the dichotomy when she writes, "Pippin's innate cheerfulness, for instance, becomes heroic optimism on multiple occasions: he is not immune from despair, but he never succumbs to it."[129]

These Hobbits are "a far cry from the comical, bumbling Hobbits of Jackson's movies," as Amendt-Raduege puts it.[130] In the movies, they are mainly there for comedic relief, but the actual characters offer far more depth than that. In fact, the books make it clear that both would have gone all the way to Mordor with Frodo and Sam, should they have been afforded the opportunity. They recognized this from the beginning, when Merry first began conspiring ways to get Frodo out of the Shire.

....

128   Flieger, "The Curious Incident," 99–112.

129   Amendt-Raduege, "A Seed of Courage," 4.

130   Ibid., 7.

APPLYING THE WISDOM OF HOBBITS: LIFE IS MESSY

What do the stories of all these characters teach us? If we are paying attention, plenty! Like Hobbits, we are complex creatures. Each and every one of us has the capability to be the most loving, forgiving, merciful, and noble person alive, and yet we all have our dark sides as well. We all struggle against our internal demons in one way or another, but what Tolkien helps elucidate for us is that when we fail—as some (wrongly) say Frodo did—we can still be seen as heroic, even if we, like Sam, don't see ourselves as such.

After all, we are all a work in progress. We are messy. We, like many Hobbits, have suffered trauma, and as we all know, trauma of any kind can be debilitating and long-lasting. Gollum, for instance, suffered for 500 years before falling to his death alongside the Ring. Frodo's suffering was much shorter, but it was traumatic nonetheless. Either way, the only thing we can do is show empathy by offering pity and mercy on others when their trauma incapacitates their mind and body.

Of course, pity and mercy are not synonyms for trustworthiness. Gollum was never to be trusted, though he could be shown empathy. So, it is for many of us. We have people in our lives who have wronged us and continue to wrong us—they should only be allowed to get so close. But they too can be shown mercy when they are at their darkest. Balance is the key here; show a sense of mercy to those who can't be trusted, but do not let them close enough to hurt you.

For those whom we do trust, however, empathy and mercy must still be present. This is because as we mentioned in this chapter's opening, not even heroes start out as heroes.[131] Everyone is in progress. We are all at different points along the adventure called life, and whether you are just outside the borders of the Shire or the walls of Mordor, your life matters. Have patience with yourself, because as a wise sage once said, "It's a dangerous business, Frodo, going out of your door. You step into the Road, and if you don't keep your feet, there is no knowing where you might be swept off to."[132]

What I take this to mean is that, among other things, life is dangerous and it takes guts to put yourself out there. Sometimes, it would be easier just to hang out at The Ivy Bush and gossip with the others. But to stay stuck in that kind of life is to miss the beauty, wonder, and awe of Middle-earth. Our messy but extraordinary Hobbit heroes chose a different life, and it is one we can all choose. None of us are beyond redemption, none of us are too small or insignificant, and it is never too late to be a hero. As their tales from Middle-earth teach us, sometimes the biggest heroes don't wear capes and armor, nor do they wield a broadsword; instead, they wear green and yellow tunics, walk around on bare feet, and can still surprise us decades after thinking we've learned all their ways.

. . . .

131 Ibid., 4.

132 Tolkien, *The Fellowship of the Ring*, 82.

·· 6 ··
free will in light of the providence of ilúvatar

"*Elrond raised his eyes and looked at him, and Frodo felt his heart pierced by the sudden keenness of the glance. 'If I understand aright all that I have heard,' he said, 'I think that this task is appointed for you, Frodo; and that if you do not find a way, no one will. This is the hour of the Shire-folk, when they arise from their quiet fields to shake the towers and counsels of the Great. Who of all the Wise could have foreseen it? Or, if they are wise, why should they expect to know it, until the hour has struck? But it is a heavy burden. So heavy that none could lay it on another. I do not lay it on you. But if you take it freely, I will say that your choice is right; and though all the mighty elf-friends of old, Hador, and Húrin, and Túrin, and Beren himself were assembled together, your seat should be among them.'*"[133]

— FROM "THE COUNCIL OF ELROND," IN
THE FELLOWSHIP OF THE RING

....

133 Tolkien, *The Fellowship of the Ring*, 303–4.

Philosophers have been debating the nature of free will for ages; from Plato and Aristotle to Descartes and Kant, all the way to moderns like Sam Harris, David Bentley Hart, Ric Machuga, Eric Reitan, and Thomas Talbott, philosophers have been constantly arguing over the nature of human volition, how it has shaped and molded the world, and even how it has impacted the ways in which we think about God and our relation to the divine. Because of this, it will hardly be my intention to put forth a thesis-level understanding of free will that finally settles the score (as if that could even be accomplished!). Further, because Tolkien himself isn't exactly explicit in his understanding of how free will "works" in Middle-earth—there are various, highly nuanced views found throughout his Legendarium—this chapter will be more of an exploration of how he uses the themes of fate and choice, rather than a definitive answer to the question at hand. (A caveat, however: we *will be* making a few philosophical assumptions, which we'll discuss shortly.) Because this is primarily a book about how a certain diminutive race called Hobbits can impact us in positive ways, we will apply all these themes to how we view our world, in hopes that we can approach others with more empathy, compassion, and ultimately, love—because isn't that the point? To love one another as Sam loved Frodo, as Arwen loved Aragorn, and as Beren loved Lúthien?

SOME PHILOSOPHICAL PRESUPPOSITIONS

Before getting into the meat of this chapter, I wanted to first define our terms and admit some of the philosophical presuppositions we will be having with regards to free will. Then and only then can we start exploring Tolkien's world.

When most Western people think of the term "free will," they imagine someone who is able to "freely" choose one course of action from another, or even many "anothers." For instance, if you want potatoes for dinner, you can freely choose to boil 'em, mash 'em, or stick 'em in a stew. *You have the free will.* But this basic understanding is quite limited and, so far as I'm aware, has been rejected by most philosophers, who all agree that a truly robust definition of free will includes some mention of the purposive forces that drive our choices. As philosopher David Bentley Hart puts it, "The will is, of its nature, teleological, and every rational act is intrinsically purposive, prompted by some final cause."[134] In other words, the will does not spontaneously choose one course of action over others in the name of profoundly libertarian freedom[135]; it is drawn by some end, real or imagined. Hart continues: "One cannot so much as freely stir a finger without the lure of some aim, proximate or remote, great or small, constant or evanescent."[136]

What this means is that our wills are influenced by any number of factors. First, as Hart rightly argues, it is drawn by final cause of some sort—we opt to mash our potatoes over sticking them in a stew because we like the textural difference between mashed potatoes and whatever we happen to be eating alongside it. Second, and of even more significance, our wills are drawn by some sense of moral

. . . .

134 Bentley Hart, *The Experience of God*, 240.

135 When I use the term "libertarian," I am not talking about the political philosophy of libertarianism. Rather, I am referring to how German philosopher Immanuel Kant described—erroneously, I must admit—human volition as "the absolute spontaneity of the will." (Kant, *Religion*, 19)

136 Bentley Hart, *The Experience of God*, 240.

responsibility—perhaps not when it comes to potatoes, but other, more impactful decisions: to do the morally good thing or to reject it.

Of course, as we all know, we often fail to choose "the good." Many will attribute this to using one's own "free will" to choose evil, but as many others have rightly argued, this is a bit of a misnomer. Once again, here's Hart:

> On any cogent account, free will is a power inherently purposive, teleological, primordially oriented toward *the good*, and shaped by that transcendental appetite to the degree that a soul can recognize the good for what it is [...] To see the good truly is to desire it insatiably; not to desire it is not to have known it, and so never to have been free to choose it (my emphasis).[137]

What Hart is saying here, though linguistically complex, is quite simple: to be truly free is to be free from the blinders that prevent us from doing the morally good action. To put it another way: to fail in doing the morally good action is to presuppose some kind of bondage. Or, if you like, Protestant theologian Karl Barth once put it like this: "Disobedience is not a choice, but the incapacity of the man who is no longer or not yet able to choose in real freedom."[138] And finally, as professor of English literature, Donald T. Williams, puts it:

> We find the essence of our humanity, our identity as children of Ilúvatar, in those moments when [...] we show our freedom within the bounds of the world by choosing the right.[139]

. . . .

137   Hart, "God, Creation, and Evil," 10.

138   Barth, *Church Dogmatics II.2*, 779.

139   Williams, *Mere Humanity*, 125.

Of course, the obvious question is raised: what prevents everyone from choosing the morally good action? The answer, however, will have to wait until later because first we need to go all the way back to the beginning, to the creation of Middle-earth. This will lay the foundation for the rest of our discussion.

"IN THE BEGINNING"

With some of our philosophical definitions and presuppositions out of the way, we can now begin our exploration of Tolkien's themes by going all the way back to the start, namely, to *The Silmarillion*.

The Silmarillion begins with Tolkien's creation myth, the Ainulindalë. In this tale, Eru Ilúvatar (God) creates the Ainur (the Holy Ones, equivalent to most people's concept of angels) and then teaches them musical themes that build and resolve, eventually becoming disharmonious, dissonant, and tense for reasons we will discuss shortly. It is through this music—as dissonant as it is—that the physical world (Arda)—as dissonant and full of suffering as it sometimes is—comes to be. In other words, the physical world, including Middle-earth and all that dwells on it, is a manifestation of the Music of the Ainur.

So, what does this Music teach us about Ilúvatar? Is Eru as dissonant as the music suggests? Is he to be trusted? Is he wise? Good? Or, malevolent like Sauron? The cause of suffering and evil? No matter how we answer, these questions will impact how we think about the relationship between Eru and the Hobbits he created, and specifically how their free will comes into play.

THE FALL AND EVENTUAL REDEMPTION

The answer to the question of Eru's dissonance is complicated. On the one hand, let me first start by saying that Eru isn't the creator of suffering and evil. He isn't the singer of the dissonant countermelody. However, he *is* somewhat responsible in that he created the being who is—Melkor (later known as Morgoth). But he is *responsible-with-a-twist*, as it were. Here's Ilúvatar's response to Melkor's disharmonious musical contribution.

> "Mighty are the Ainur, and mightiest among them is Melkor; but that he may know, and all the Ainur, that I am Ilúvatar, those things that ye have sung, I will show them forth, that ye may see what ye have done. And thou, Melkor, shalt see that no theme may be played that hath not its uttermost source in me, nor can any alter the music in my despite. For he that attempteth this shall prove but mine instrument in the devising of things more wonderful, which he himself hath not imagined."[140]

So, think of it like this: Melkor is trying to create dissonance in the melody, but in even creating that, the resolve (ending the melody back on the one-chord) will be ever more stunning and satisfying after such a harsh and discordant sound (musicians know this!). In other words, in attempting to destroy the melody of Ilúvatar, Melkor only makes the ending more beautiful; and while Ilúvatar does not condone evil, he will create something good in spite of it[141] (as later prophecies

. . . .

140   Tolkien, *The Silmarillion*, 6.

141   A discussion about theodicy—any response to the question, "How can a good God exist in a world full of so much evil and suffering?"—would generally be appropriate here, but it will have to wait until later in the chapter.

about the Second Music of the Ainur would suggest).[142] Of course, how he accomplishes the redemption of Arda is a bit of a mystery, though we do have some evidence of precisely how his hand works. In *The Silmarillion*, Tolkien tells us the following:

> Even as the first shadows were felt in Mirkwood there appeared in the west of Middle-earth the Istari, whom Men called the Wizards. None knew at that time whence they were, save Círdan of the Havens, and only to Elrond and to Galadriel did he reveal that they came over the Sea. But afterwards it was said among the Elves that they were messengers sent by the Lords of the West to contest the power of Sauron, if he should rise again, and to move Elves and Men and all living things of good will to valiant deeds.[143]

In other words, the Istari—of which Gandalf was one—were the "hands and feet" of Eru, responsible for inspiring others to choose "the good," especially when bravery would be needed to do so.

. . . .

142 There are multiple prophecies about a Second Music of the Ainur, which are sung without any dissonance whatsoever, suggesting a most hopeful ending for the entire creation. The first comes from "Of the Beginning of Days," which reads: "But Melkor has cast his shadow upon it, and confounded it with darkness, and brought forth evil out of good, and fear out of hope. Yet of old the Valar declared to the Elves of Valinor that Men shall join in the Second Music of the Ainur; whereas Ilúvatar has not revealed what he purposes for the Elves after the World's end, and Melkor has not discovered it." (Tolkien, *The Silmarillion*, 36) The second comes from something Tom Bombadil once said: "Lost and forgotten be, darker than the darkness, where gates stand forever shut, till the World is mended." (Tolkien, *The Lord of the Rings*, 162) The third comes from a conversation and debate between an elf called Finrod and a human woman called Andreth. After a lengthy discussion, Finrod says the following: "If we are indeed the Eruhin, the Children of the One, then He will not suffer Himself to be deprived of His own, not by any Enemy, not even by ourselves." (Tolkien, *The History of Middle-earth: Morgoth's Ring*, "Athrabeth Finrod Ah Andreth")

143 Tolkien, *The Silmarillion*, 357–58.

Now, at this point you may be asking yourself: Does this mean that Tolkien's characters do not have free will? If it is foreordained that Ilúvatar should have a specific happy ending play out—if it is *fated* to be—does that mean all our favorite characters are mere pawns on his divine chessboard? In the section that follows, we'll discuss how that is not at all what is going on in the text, and why both Ilúvatar's plan for redemption and his created order's free will—Hobbits and Humans, most specifically[144]—can coexist.

FATE & FREE WILL: STRIKING A BALANCE

Early on in this chapter, we established that free will is not merely choosing between two or more actions; rather, it bears with it some sort of moral responsibility and is driven by some final cause, real or imagined. Most philosophers of whom I'm aware argue for such a thing. Some take it further and suggest that the truly *freed* will is the one that chooses the good (whatever that happens to be at any given point). I tend to agree with them, and believe that is exactly what is going on in Middle-earth, too.

Why is this important?

Because it means that both fate and free will can work in tandem, alongside chance, to bring about Ilúvatar's end.

You see, when Ilúvatar creates the world, he doesn't simply create a beginning and let everything go from there. Using the music analogy

. . . .

144   Since this is a book primarily about Hobbits, our focus will be on them,
       rather than on *all* the races in Middle-earth. The reasons being: Elves and
       Dwarves may have a different level, or even type, of free will, as compared
       to Hobbits. We discuss Men alongside Hobbits because Hobbits are
       descendants of them and thus, are more alike than the other races.

again, as the Writer and Composer, he has the entire piece in mind; he just gives all the players the chance to "solo" during portions of it. During this "soloing," choices are made. Sometimes notes are played that fall out of alignment with the overarching theme of the music, but as time goes by, the piece builds and builds until the fated final resolve—the redemption and reconciliation of Arda.

No more does this ring true (pardon the pun), than when Gandalf is consoling Frodo about the Ring being handed to him.

> "Behind that there was something else at work, beyond any design of the Ring-maker. I can put it no plainer than by saying that Bilbo was *meant* to find the Ring, and *not* by its maker. In which case you were also *meant* to have it. And that may be an encouraging thought."[145]

The obvious question is raised: who or what force of good did this? The implication is that it is Eru Ilúvatar himself who brings the Ring to Bilbo and Frodo. But that is not explicitly said in the text. In fact, nothing more is said than what we just quoted. It's simply said that both Bilbo and Frodo were *meant* to have the Ring, and that fact should be of comfort to a trembling Frodo. What we can infer, however, is that whatever force brought the Ring to Frodo should be thought of as a comfort, as it had good intentions, and there is none as good as Ilúvatar.

Free will comes into play a short time later, when Gandalf presents Frodo with *the* choice—what to do about the Ring? At first, Frodo does not know. He desires to save the Shire, but also feels "very small, and very uprooted, and well—desperate."[146] But then, the "good" presents itself to Frodo and the choice becomes a non-choice: "a great

....

145 Tolkien, *The Fellowship of the Ring*, 61.

146 Ibid., 69.

desire to follow Bilbo flamed up in his heart [...] It was so strong that it overcame his fear: he could almost have run out there and then down the road without his hat, as Bilbo had done on a similar morning long ago."[147]

Later in the journey, Frodo makes a similar free choice. After a lengthy discussion—lengthy doesn't even begin to describe it accurately—the Council of Elrond stands at an impasse. *What to do about the Ring?* Finally, Frodo decides for them: "I will take the Ring."[148] From there, Elrond puts forth two seemingly juxtaposed ideas that work in tandem when thinking about the balance between fate and free will in the way we've been exploring. On the one hand, Elrond suggests that it is fate that leads Frodo to be in the position he came to: "I think this task is appointed for you, Frodo; and that if you do not find a way, no one will."[149] On the other, he explicitly states that it is Frodo's "free" choice that he is to make: "But it is a heavy burden. So heavy that none could lay it on another. I do not lay it on you. But if you take it freely, I will say that your choice is right."[150]

As we all know, the right choice is indeed made. Frodo decides to continue to bear the burden of the Ring all the way to Mordor, and in the end, saves all of Middle-earth. And while it was fated to be this way, it was fated in such a way where Frodo's free will—a will that is directed towards the goodness of Ilúvatar—becomes the means by which everything comes to pass.

....

147   Ibid.

148   Ibid., 303.

149   Ibid.

150   Ibid., 304.

EVIL CHOICES ABOUND

Finally, we come to the place where we ask the inevitable, "yeah, but what about evil and suffering?"

In Tolkien's Middle-earth, evil is certainly something with which the characters must contend. And whether he takes what is called a Manichean view—where evil is a very real and concrete thing—or a Boethian view[151]—where evil is the privation of something good—evil is experienced by every character in Middle-earth.

The question for *us* to contend with is *why*?

The mythological answer from *The Silmarillion* is that Melkor begins singing a dissonant melody during the Music of the Ainur. But while this is a poetic and esoteric way of explaining evil and suffering, more concrete answers still need to be explored. After all, does it fully make sense to start in on a discussion about dissonant countermelodies, for instance, if we are attempting to answer why Sméagol instantly succumbs to the power of the Ring, while Sam is able to freely give it back to Frodo? Again, these mythological and analogical explanations can be helpful (to a degree), but more practical language is often needed.

So, why *does* Sméagol succumb to its power?

That's a difficult question to answer, and one Tolkien doesn't explicitly state. We are indeed told that Sméagol immediately desires the Ring that Déagol found, but immediately desiring something does not have to lead to murder. In fact, most of the time it doesn't.

. . . .

151 My friend and retired philosophy professor, Ric Machuga, had this
to say in a recent email exchange: "While it is certainly true that
Boethius argued that evil is a privation, this understanding of evil
goes back much further to at least Plato. And in Christian circles,
it goes back to at least Augustine and Gregory of Nyssa."

There was something already corrupt and sinister within Sméagol that leads him to kill his closest friend.

Tolkien says as much. While explaining the Ring's backstory, Gandalf tells Frodo that, "he was interested in roots and beginnings; he dived into deep pools; he burrowed under trees and growing plants; he tunnelled into green mounds; and he ceased to look up at the hilltops, or the leaves on trees, or the flowers opening in the air: his head and his eyes were downward."[152]

NATURE VS. NURTURE

There are two reasons as to why Sméagol is like this. The first is that it is simply in his nature: What is his "DNA" made of? How is he wired? What is his personality like? Does he have a natural proclivity to desire power? The second is that he had been brought up this way: How had he been punished as a young Stoorish Hobbit? Was there compassion found in his home? Did he suffer childhood traumas?

The reality is that Sméagol is who he is for both reasons. It is built into his fabric *and* life's circumstances have moved him in that direction. That is how it seems to work for all of us, so it makes sense in the case of Sméagol. On the one hand, we all have a genetic predisposition toward certain behaviors and personality types, but on the other, our experiences shape and mold us in the most powerful of ways. For Sméagol, we are told that he was raised by a rich and reputable family in which a stern, bordering on severe, matriarch was the head. Perhaps this has impacted Sméagol in negative ways. We can't be certain because not much about Sméagol's past is known. But since we know Sméagol's fate and much of his personality, we can

....

152 Ibid., 57.

deduce that *something*—perhaps even something subconsciously— has coerced him to become who he will become: an enslaved shell of his original innocent self.

The question, then, is this: does Sméagol have free will? Well, yes. And no. And maybe; we can't be one-hundred-percent sure, and it probably depends upon when you ask. On the one hand, all Humans and Hobbits—children of Ilúvatar—are given free will by Eru. That much we know. But on the other hand, Sméagol is enslaved by the Ring. To that end, Sméagol's free will—everyone's free will, for that matter—*can be thought of as a spectrum*. The freest beings—those not enslaved by something like the Ring or the desire for power—utilize their free will to choose "the good." The most enslaved beings— Gollum, Saruman, and Wormtongue—perhaps have had a level of free will at some point, but because of a number of different contributing factors, lose their freedom in their pursuit of power.

A HUMBLE THEODICY

Okay, so back to searching for concrete answers to the problem of evil. Asked this way: *If Eru is good, why is there so much suffering in Middle-earth?* Well, as we alluded to earlier, because Melkor introduced evil into the world, and evil always leads to suffering. But why do both persist in a world held together by Eru?

The answer I'm inclined to provide, while simple, seems the most accurate: without evil, we never get *The Lord of the Rings*. As it pertains to Hobbits, perhaps we get some gardening tips, a recipe for roasted conies, and a how-to guide for blowing smoke rings. A very fine read, but not an adventure that continues to stand the test of time.

Of course, in the face of suffering, *an answer like this hardly suffices*. But be honest! Does any answer suffice? Of course not. The best we can do—Tolkien included—is to dare to hope that in spite of evil and suffering, a good tale can be spun on our way to redemption.

And perhaps that's the key—we approach the suffering experienced in Middle-earth from the end looking back. The end of *The Lord of the Rings* is a happy one. All fairy tales are. But even more than that, and as we discussed earlier, there is strong evidence throughout Tolkien's Legendarium of a *fully* restored and redeemed Arda (represented by a Second Music of the Ainur) that comes prior to the end of time. And so, any current suffering, no matter how small or how horrific, eventually gets redeemed by Ilúvatar, and that should at least bring us some comfort.

APPLYING THE WISDOM OF HOBBITS: EMPATHY, PITY, & MERCY

Why does all of this philosophical talk matter?

First, it matters because it allows us to show others pity, mercy even. Frodo, following in the footsteps of his uncle Bilbo, has pity on Gollum. Both have mercy on him when they could have chosen violence. But they must recognize the enslavement Sméagol faces— trapped by the Ring's seduction, forced to live in torment, crawling and lurking across the ground in pursuit of only one thing—and in doing so choose to compassionately spare his life.

Piggybacking on that, all this matters because it allows us to have compassion for ourselves. All of us are works in progress, being pulled this way and that, as we try to seek goodness, truth, and love. Many times, we come up short. This is inevitable. But knowing that there will be chances to get back up again and turn towards the good in life makes all the difference. We are not statically fixed and rigid; we can grow toward having greater freedom to choose the good.

Lastly, being that there is ample evidence that all children of Ilúvatar are fated to experience a blissful end, we can rest assured that our free choices which lead us there actually matter. Life in Middle-earth is difficult, sometimes bleak even, and many souls are born into impossible circumstances, but having the knowledge that we can impact our fate in positive ways can only lead us toward experiencing more pleasure and less pain.

There needs to be balance, however. What Hobbits also teach us is that we *are* our brother's keeper. We are responsible for ourselves, but we are also responsible for others. These aren't mutually exclusive notions. And so, those who end up making choices that lead to their eventual enslavement bear responsibility, but as a community, we also bear some as well.

PART III

....

hobbit wisdom

Slip away, dear Frodo,
Across the Sundering Seas.
I'll be home, dear Frodo,
Elanor's waiting for me.

·· 7 ··

when returning home is not an option

"Then Frodo kissed Merry and Pippin, and last of all Sam, and went aboard; and the sails were drawn up, and the wind blew, and slowly the ship slipped away down the long grey firth; and the light of the glass of Galadriel that Frodo bore glimmered and was lost. And the ship went out into the High Sea and passed on into the West, until at last on a night of rain Frodo smelled a sweet fragrance on the air and heard the sound of singing that came over the water." [153]

— FROM "THE GREY HAVENS," IN *THE RETURN OF THE KING*

❧

....

153 Tolkien, *The Return of the King*, 339.

Throughout their history, Hobbits have bravely sacrificed much. During the so-called "Long Winter," for example, where Hobbits starved and froze to death by the thousands, their valor is so profound that hundreds of years later Gandalf continues to talk about it.[154] And who can forget our old friend, Bandobras "Bullroarer" Took, who risked his own life as he saved the Shire from the goblin invasion in T.A. 2747? But nowhere is sacrifice better seen on full display than when Frodo decides to save the Shire (by saving all of Middle-earth), despite knowing full-well he may not make it out alive.

Frodo is not the only Hobbit among the Fellowship who sacrifices his own well-being for the sake and benefit of others, however. As we have explored all throughout this book, every Hobbit within the Fellowship—Frodo, Sam, Merry, Pippin, and even Fatty[155]—gives up something in order to "step out onto the Road," as it were. And in doing so, they all gain and lose something—some more than others—and none of them return the same.

WHAT WE MEAN BY "SACRIFICE"

Now, before we get too far ahead of ourselves by discussing the bravery of Frodo, Sam, and the others, let's first talk about the word "sacrifice." Because this is a very loaded term, it's best to define what we mean.

No doubt, "sacrifice" has been used in several ways, initially to describe archaic religions and their practice of spilling blood in order

· · · · · · · · · · · · · · · · · · ·

154 Tolkien, J.R.R., and Tolkien, Christopher.
Unfinished Tales, "The Quest of Erebor."

155 After Frodo leaves Buckland, his friend Fatty Bolger stays
behind and in doing so, keeps the Black Riders from catching
up with the other four Hobbits while in the wilderness.

to receive blessings and boons from the gods. But as you likely figured out by reading the first two paragraphs of this chapter, that is not how we are using the term here, and not just because Hobbits are a secular society through and through. Instead, we are talking about sacrifice in the context of putting aside one's safety, comfort, and well-being for the benefit of others—a self-sacrifice of sorts.

But don't think of sacrifice as an act that is done for notoriety or for the desire to be some sort of hero—Hobbits, contrary to the Big Folk, rarely (if ever) think in these terms. Instead, Hobbits sacrifice their own well-being specifically *because* of their love of fellowship, their love of their fellow Hobbit. Whereas Men tend to sacrifice themselves for others because it's the honorable thing to do—I'm reminded of someone like Boromir or even Beren long ago—Hobbits do so without such pretenses. Devoid of any quid pro quo, they step into uncomfortable situations solely for the love of others, the love of the Shire, and the love of what it means to be a Hobbit. Nowhere is this clearer than in the story of Frodo Baggins.

SAVE THE SHIRE, BUT NOT FOR ME

"Well, here at last, dear friends, on the shores of the Sea comes the end of our fellowship in Middle-earth. Go in peace! I will not say: do not weep; for not all tears are an evil."[156]

— Gandalf

Though we all probably love Frodo, his story is not a pleasant one. While it ends happily enough—albeit quite bittersweet—his journey

....

156 Tolkien, *The Return of the King*, 339.

isn't enjoyable. Not for the reader, nor the character himself. In fact, after the events of the first chapter of *The Fellowship of the Ring*, we only get glimpses of the *happy-go-lucky, enjoy a beer and a party* Frodo. Most of the time, it's the burdened, troubled, and distressed version.

We all know why. From the beginning, Frodo knows the peril he is in. He knows from the moment he is presented with the Ring by Gandalf that everything in his life will be altered. In fact, even his beloved Shire, the thing he has loved the most, is at risk of being lost to him: "I feel that as long as the Shire lies behind, safe and comfortable, I shall find wandering more bearable: I shall know that somewhere there is a firm foothold, even if my feet cannot stand there again."[157]

As we find out toward the end of *The Return of the King*, Frodo's feet indeed stand in the Shire again, though not on firm ground. And though he stays in the Shire a year or so after the end of the War of the Ring—cleaning up loose ends and lending a helping hand in and around Bag End—he eventually acknowledges that the Shire will not and cannot be saved for him. Though the Hobbits have restored and rebuilt it after its razing, Frodo's personal wounds run too deep. He finally realizes that peace can only be had outside of it (in Valinor, to be exact).

This is the bittersweet part of Frodo's ending. He is the main catalyst—though perhaps not the main "hero"[158]—for the salvation of the Shire, and yet, because of the wounds he suffered in his sacrifice for others, he is never able to enjoy it again.

. . . .

157 Tolkien, *The Fellowship of the Ring*, 68.

158 Tolkien contends—and as a gardener myself, I fully agree with him—that Samwise Gamgee is the chief hero of *The Lord of the Rings* (see "Letter #131" in *The Letters of J.R.R. Tolkien*).

But it's not just his literal wounds that are the cause of his suffering. Sure, he still has shoulder pain from the Morgul blade that pierced his flesh. But that's the superficial pain, the kind you can rub an ointment on or drink a tea for. It's the deep existential pain—the kind you only get from sacrificially bearing something as burdensome as the Ring for as long as Frodo did—that causes him to have to eventually leave Middle-earth, his friends, the Shire, Bag End, and everything else he has loved so dearly. As he explains to Sam just prior to their parting:

> I have been too deeply hurt, Sam. I tried to save the Shire, and it has been saved, but not for me. It must often be so, Sam, when things are in danger: some one has to give them up, lose them, so that others may keep them. But you are my heir: all that I had and might have had I leave to you.[159]

And so, Frodo leaves Sam behind to continue the work they started together.

This is the type of sacrifice we discussed in the previous section, where one person gives up something for another to gain it—not to be called a hero, or to pass on a family lineage of honor, valor, and pride, but solely for the people you love. And that is precisely the word Frodo would use: Love. Frodo loves the Shire and its furry-footed inhabitants—none more so than Sam—and will continue to love the Shire even as he heads west across the Sundering Seas.[160]

....

159 Tolkien, *The Return of the King*, 338.

160 The Sundering Seas, or Belegaer, are the seas that lay between Aman in the west and Middle-earth in the east.

SAM EVENTUALLY HEADS WEST

Unlike Frodo's story, Sam's is less bitter, a little sweeter, but still full of sacrifice nonetheless. In fact, like Frodo, Sam gives up *everything* he had ever known to head east.

Though not a famous Hobbit before their adventure, Sam is certainly a comfortable one. He's a gardener—and a good one at that—a lover of poetry, a rope maker, and a brother to five siblings whom he has lived with alongside his father on Bagshot Row (a nearly perfect life if you ask me). And yet, there is also something inside Sam that makes him put aside all these comforts the minute Frodo needs him.

In fact, though Sam hears Gandalf and Frodo discussing the terrors that may befall them on their journey—"an enemy, and rings, and dragons, and a fiery mountain"[161]—he does not delay in accepting their call to adventure, as well as his call to be a protector of Frodo, the Ring Bearer: "'Me, sir!' cried Sam, springing up like a dog invited for a walk. 'Me go and see Elves and all! Hooray!' he shouted, and then burst into tears."[162]

For the next year or so, Sam stays true to his word, and to his friend. Though the Fellowship faces trials and tribulations—even the

. . . .

161   Tolkien, *The Fellowship of the Ring*, 70.

162   Ibid., 71.

deaths of two of their members[163]—Sam sticks with Frodo through thick and thin, even humbly and begrudgingly bearing the burden of the Ring after he believes Frodo has been killed by Shelob near the pass of Cirith Ungol.

So, what does this tell us? Two things.

First, Sam Gamgee should be counted among the bravest Hobbits in history for sacrificially giving up everything to support his friend. He should be seen as the epitome of what it means to be an extraordinary Hobbit—humble, unassuming, curious, loyal, and courageous and brave. Second, that Frodo's sacrifice was not in vain.

Though Frodo will only stay in the Shire for less than two years after their return, Sam, because of his friend's bravery, ends up leading a long, happy life with his wife, Rosie, and their thirteen children. He is gifted Bag End and the *Red Book of Westmarch* and given the name "Gardner" to honor him for restoring the Shire after it had been laid to waste by Saruman and his minions. Additionally, he will also go on to serve as Mayor of the Shire for seven consecutive 7-year terms, even earning the revered Star of the Dúnedain from King Elessar.

But like everything in Middle-earth, heartbreak will finally come. In year 61 of the Fourth Age, Rosie will pass away, which in turn

. . . .

163   I'm referring to Boromir, who died near the banks of the Anduin River, and Gandalf the Grey, who vanished into the abyss near the Bridge of Khazad-dûm. Because Gandalf later returns as Gandalf the White, many think he did not die. And technically, perhaps he didn't. However, after his battle and subsequent victory over the Balrog, Gandalf's spirit—being one of the Maiar of Valinor—left his body and was not reincarnated (so to speak) until later.

causes Sam to leave the Shire for good to follow Frodo into the Undying Lands.[164]

THE WISDOM OF LOSS

One thing we can take away from both Frodo and Sam's stories is this: all suffer loss. Though we may lead long, happy lives in our homes in whatever version of Hobbiton we reside, eventually loss will come knocking on our door. Sam tastes it when his beloved Rosie, the mother of his thirteen children, dies. But he also tastes loss when Frodo leaves him some decades prior. To that end, no matter how suffering and loss find us, they will find us sooner or later.

And so, the question we must ask ourselves is this: what can we do about it? How can we prepare for such loss? Initially, three bits of Hobbit wisdom spring to mind.

APPRECIATING WHAT WE HAVE

Because we will suffer in life, it's best to appreciate what we have, no matter how much or how little. Notice the small things—the smell of the flowers and shrubs as you walk down the lane, the taste of pipe-weed as you blow your smoke rings, the feeling of the soil between your fingers as you tend to your plants, the sensation you get cozied up near a fire on a cold, rainy autumn evening. These are the things that color our lives when all our adventures are behind (or ahead of) us. What we may initially think of as the mundane truly are things that keep us grounded in appreciation of what is right in front of us.

. . . .

164 Sam was able to join Frodo in the West because, though brief, he indeed carried the Ring for a time.

Moreover, enjoy these "mundane" things with the people around you. Take walks with others. Stroll through the park. Smoke pipe-weed with your friends, like Gandalf and Bilbo used to do. Share a garden together with your comrade in life, like Michael Machuga and I do. Because when you do, you'll realize that these are the memories that will last throughout your days. What will last won't be your collections or your so-called valuables; it won't be the treasures you dug up from under the Lonely Mountain. Your most prized memories will be those moments in time you spend fellowshipping with friends.

HOLDING LOOSELY TO THAT WHICH WE LOVE

If we don't hold loosely to what we have, to what we love, we will be distraught whenever we face loss. While suffering in the midst of loss is inevitable, holding too tightly will never ease our burdens. And so, a part of "growing up," of being spiritually mature, is to learn to let go, as Frodo has, even prior to first stepping out onto the Road. "I feel that as long as the Shire lies behind, safe and comfortable, I shall find wandering more bearable: I shall know that somewhere there is a firm foothold, even if my feet cannot stand there again."[165]

Of course, this doesn't mean we diminish our love for the things, places, and people in our lives. In fact, the reality is quite the opposite. When we learn to hold loosely to those things and people that mean the most to us, we allow them to "breathe," so to speak. Holding loosely allows those things to be what they are without us having to impress upon them. To love them is to give them some space.

. . . .

165 Tolkien, *The Fellowship of the Ring*, 68.

Moreover, as Franciscan priest, Fr. Richard Rohr, once noticed, "All mature spirituality is about letting go."[166]

As I just said, Frodo experiences this, but so did Sam, Merry, Pippin, and so many others. All have had to hold loosely to the Shire, their homes, their favorite tavern, their beloved pipe-weed, their mushrooms, and their friends and family in order to save those very things, and we would be wise to follow suit in our own lives.

EMBRACING THE BEAUTIFUL PRESENT MOMENT

Finally, we all must learn to embrace the present moment, as that is all we really have. Sure, we have wonderful memories of shared moments with fellow Hobbits. We also have grand plans for our future—goals, accomplishments, achievements. But the reality is that neither the past nor the future exist. Only the present exists, and if we spend too much time reminiscing about the past or ruminating about the future, we'll miss the nasturtians that are right in front of our noses.

The Shire is the perfect place to slow down and be present. But that doesn't mean you need to travel all the way to Middle-earth to discover it. The Shire can exist in your very midst. If you are at home cooking or eating a plate of mushrooms and bacon, slow down and be present with your food. Taste every bite. Feel the texture of the ingredients. If you are puttering around in your garden, stop to smell the fragrant flowers, notice the different colors of the plants, watch for butterflies and hummingbirds. And when you are with your fellow Hobbits sharing a pint or a smoke, really be there with them. Put the events of the day behind you and really soak in the fellowship. If you

. . . .

166 Rohr, *Breathing Under Water*, 6.

fail to do these things, you'll miss the point of what this life is for—to be present in the moments we have right in front of us.

APPLYING THE WISDOM OF HOBBITS: LIVE IN THE NOW

Too often, life is wrought with peril, with evil, with suffering. Often, the places we once called home can no longer be that for us. So, we have to move on. But when we do, we can take the positive memories with us and carry them wherever we go, not pining for or longing for them to return to us, but just to have them alongside us as we continue to be present and aware of our immediate surroundings. Though life may be a bittersweet realization, as it is for Frodo, sometimes holding life loosely is all that can be done. Though we may weep, finding ourselves buried under the weight of emotion that comes with loss, Gandalf's words are always there as a reminder to us: "not all tears are an evil."[167] Though they may feel like it at the time, it doesn't have to remain that way.

After Sam returns to the Shire, I'm certain that he quickly realizes this. No doubt, the parting of his best friend has been a bitter pill to swallow. But he still has his family—his Rosie Cotton and their thirteen children—he still has his garden and his home in Bag End (given to him by Frodo), and he still has a long, storied future in the Shire. But for Sam to be content with these things, he has to hold loosely to his relationship with Frodo. He has to appreciate their time together as well as the time that will pass by until their next meeting, years later in the Blessed Realms of Valinor.

. . . .

167   Tolkien, *The Return of the King*, 339.

·· 8 ··

From the ashes, a shire reborn

"'They've cut it down!' cried Sam. 'They've cut down the Party Tree!' He pointed to where the tree had stood under which Bilbo had made his Farewell Speech. It was lying lopped and dead in the field. As if this was the last straw Sam burst into tears."[168]

— FROM "THE SCOURING OF THE SHIRE"
IN *THE RETURN OF THE KING*

꒱

....

168 Tolkien, *The Return of the King*, 322.

L ike Sam, we've all faced heartbreak—that feeling we get when something we've loved dearly is taken from us. So, when he, a skillful gardener[169] and lover of all things that grow, returns from his adventure with Frodo and sees the beloved Party Tree hewn down by Saruman and his ruffians, we feel his tremendous pain as it reverberates from the pages. As we read, we feel it in our bones, in our veins. From our head to our toes, and deep within our heart of hearts, his heartbreak triggers in us that gut-wrenching trauma we've all faced during our lives.

And yet, many of us have also experienced immense motivation that comes from pain and trauma—grief that gives way to an inner burning that can hardly be quenched. Sam and the other Hobbits experience this very thing after the realization that their beloved Shire has been razed, replaced by the all too familiar gears and smoke of industry.

THE SCOURING OF THE SHIRE: A BRIEF SUMMARY OF EVENTS

"It will not keep you on your road, nor defend you against any peril; but if you keep it and see your home again at last, then perhaps it may reward you. Though you should find all barren and laid waste, there will be few gardens in Middle-earth that will bloom like your garden, if you sprinkle this earth there."[170]

— Galadriel

. . . .

169 Sam was such an adept gardener that his descendants took the name "Gardner" in honor of Sam's replanting of the Shire after it was destroyed by Saruman and his ruffians.

170 Tolkien, *The Fellowship of the Ring*, 422.

After the Ring is destroyed and Sauron vanquished, and after many celebrations and final goodbyes, Frodo, Sam, Merry, and Pippin arrive at the Brandywine Bridge, the gateway into the Shire from the east. Only, nothing is how they left it. Instead of a bridge open for travelling Hobbits, it is closed with a daunting spiked gate and a frightened gatekeeper. "'Who's that? Be off! You can't come in. Can't you read the notice: *No admittance between sundown and sunrise?*'"[171]

The four Hobbits, as battle-scarred and tested as they now had become, pay little attention to this vapid admonition, and set out for Hobbiton, encountering a group of Hobbit Shirriffs along the way. The Shirriffs attempt, in vain, to arrest the four, who can't help but laugh at the ineptitude of this quasi-police force daring to stand in their way.

After a brief exchange with the Shirriffs, in which one of them gives Sam a bit of insider information that could help them in their pursuit of justice, the four companions come across a half-dozen men. These men mention that they answer to no one but a mysterious figure called "Sharkey," and all pull their swords on Frodo. Quickly, the other three Hobbits draw *their* swords and in turn drive the men away, albeit for only a brief time. After Sam rides off to find Farmer Cotton, who gathers the entire village, the men return but are utterly defeated by the rallied Hobbits.

This will not be the final battle, however. The following day, approximately 100 more men approach Hobbiton and are met by Pippin and his relatives from Buckland. An intense and bloody battle ensues, leading to the death of seventy men and nineteen Hobbits.

....

171 Tolkien, *The Return of the King*, 300.

Tragic as the Battle of Bywater is, it is the final defense between the motivated Hobbit warriors and the Chief of the ruffians.

And this is where the plot takes a surprising turn for the Hobbits (all of them except perhaps Frodo, who half suspected a twist in the tale[172]). It turns out the Chief is not really "Sharkey," but an old nemesis: Saruman. But this is not the Saruman from *The Two Towers*. Rather, it's a powerless and pitiful Saruman, a shadow of his former self, stripped of everything except for his cunning speech and forked tongue, which he attempts to use against the Hobbits by threatening to curse the very land they stand on. But as Frodo reminds his friends, "He has lost all power, save for his voice that can still daunt you and deceive you, if you let it."[173]

Frodo's leadership—his newfound confidence—leads the way in quelching Saruman's plan to deceive them and the wizard is forced to flee the Shire with his servant Wormtongue in tow. However, due to Saruman's constant belittling of the beleaguered servant, Wormtongue finally snaps, slitting Saruman's throat with a knife he has hidden, before three Hobbit arrows are loosed into Wormtongue (thus finally ending the War of the Ring).

While it was the end of the war, it was only the beginning of the cleanup efforts. As Sam gloomily admits, "I shan't call it the end, till we've cleared up the mess [...] and that'll take a lot of time and work."[174]

Sam is correct about one thing: cleaning up the Shire indeed takes a lot of work. But it takes much less time than he has anticipated.

....

172   Ibid., 324.

173   Ibid., 325.

174   Ibid., 327.

After freeing Saruman's prisoners from the Lockholes in Michel Delving—including Fredegar Bolger, Old Will Whitfoot, and Lobelia Sackville-Baggins—and driving the last of the ruffians from the Shire, the Hobbits, like bees buzzing around blossoming lavender, get to work on fixing what has been destroyed. First the Shirriff houses are demolished, the bricks being used to shore up some of the tunnels at Michel Delving. Then, the Hill, Bag End, and Bagshot Row are restored, followed by the Old Mill. Finally, after many of the holes and buildings have been fixed up properly, Sam tackles the greatest undertaking of them all—planting new saplings where the trees have been felled.

Sam will not have to do this alone, however. He still has the gift Galadriel gave him during their visit to Lothlórien, and uses it in the only way Sam knows how:

> Sam planted saplings in all the places where specially beautiful or beloved trees had been destroyed, and he put a grain of the precious dust in the soil at the root of each. He went up and down the Shire in this labor; but if he paid special attention to Hobbiton and Bywater no one blamed him. And at the end he found that he still had a little of the dust left; so he went to the Three-Farthing Stone, which is as near the center of the Shire as no matter, and cast it in the air with his blessing. The little silver nut he planted in the Party Field where the trees had once been; and he wondered what would come of it. All through winter he remained as patient as he could, and tried to restrain himself from going round constantly to see if anything was happening.[175]

The following spring, Sam discovers that something is indeed happening! Something quite extraordinary, in fact. Trees are sprouting

....

175 Ibid., 330.

and growing as if one year were twenty. A stunning Mallorn tree is forcing its way up toward the light of the sun. And all in all, 1420 of the Shire Reckoning is, in Tolkien's words, "a marvelous year."[176] But not just any type of year! It is a year unlike the Hobbits of the Shire have ever seen, as there is not only "wonderful sunshine and delicious rain, in due times and perfect measure," but, as Tolkien continues, "an air of richness and growth, and a gleam of beauty beyond that of mortal summers that flicker and pass upon Middle-earth."[177] The fruit is "so plentiful" that young Hobbits could have bathed in strawberries and cream, and the barley so fine that that year's beer will become long remembered and even a byword.[178] All in all, it is as close to perfect as anything found in all of Middle-earth and beyond.

THE IMPORTANCE OF THESE EVENTS

Beyond the unimaginable beauty brought by 1420, the Scouring of the Shire is important for a number of reasons, two of which we need to mention.

First, it shows us firsthand the true horrors of war. For Hobbits of the Shire, war has typically been something that happened "far away," on foreign shores or in foreign lands. After the events of the War of the Ring, however, they can no longer live in such ignorance; *war has come home.* Though Sauron never has stepped foot in their lands, his presence is felt there, and the Shire nearly succumbs to his power. Were it not for four brave Hobbits, it would have.

. . . .

176   Ibid., 331.

177   Ibid.

178   Ibid.

If I had to make an educated guess as to the reason J.R.R. Tolkien included this perspective, I'd simply say this: he had personal experiences that were similar. In other words, he had tacit knowledge of such a thing,[179] so he wrote about something comparable. Though we should never analogize his work—that can't be stressed enough— it's beyond reasonable to suggest that Tolkien's real-life experiences impacted how he wrote the ending of *The Lord of the Rings*. The truth of the matter is that England had suffered a similar fate as the Shire. In fact, while Tolkien was abroad fighting in WWI, Germany was busy dropping more than 5,000 bombs on towns across Britain, killing 557 and injuring another 1,358.[180] This means it is not so much an analogy, but a shared experience; Tolkien, like the Hobbits of the Shire, knew firsthand what it was like to taste war. It was a bitter taste and took years, if not decades, to rebuild and recover from.

Just as vitally important, our second lesson from the Scouring of the Shire is that it concludes our "hero's journey," also known as the monomyth. If you will recall, the final "act" in any proper journey involves the hero returning to normal life, albeit drastically changed. The Scouring of the Shire represents that return for the four companions, just as Gandalf explicitly states: "I am with you at present, but soon I shall not be. I am not coming to the Shire. You must settle its affairs yourselves; that is what you have been trained for."[181]

As we discussed in the previous section, that's exactly what the four Hobbits do—settle their affairs themselves. To complete their

....

179 Tacit knowledge is the type of knowledge that an individual gains through direct experience that is difficult to describe in words. It was coined by the Hungarian-British scientist Michael Polanyi.

180 Linning, "Bombed but not beaten."

181 Tolkien, *The Return of the King*, 298.

journeys—their Quest, if you will—they must complete all the necessary steps, one of which is to return to their homes and liberate their people. As an aside, this omission is one thing I believe Peter Jackson got wrong in his films, as it skips the crucial last step of the monomyth. Without it, we miss one of the main points of the story, which is given to us early on. When Frodo tells Gandalf he wishes to *save the Shire*, if not for himself, but for the Hobbits of whom he has become so fond. The Scouring of the Shire is also crucial in understanding Sam's heroism—incidentally, labeled the chief hero by Tolkien himself[182]—whereby he finally gets "rewarded" for taking up the heroic call to join Frodo on the Quest. If you'll notice, after all the events of the main story, even after Frodo's departure to the Undying Lands, the book doesn't end until Sam finally returns to his garden, his wife, and his baby girl on his lap in his home in a fully restored and comfortable Bag End—probably still replete with plenty of hooks and pegs for hats and coats, just as it was for Bilbo all those years ago.

APPLYING THE WISDOM OF HOBBITS: COMPLETING OUR OWN HERO'S JOURNEY

As we mentioned at the onset of this chapter, like Bilbo, Frodo, Sam, and the others, we all will face the hardships that inevitably come with adventuring, and much of the time these will lead to trauma and suffering. In 2018, that's exactly what happened to my community and me when the infamous Camp Fire ravished the Town of Paradise, California.

. . . .

182 See "Letter #131" in *The Letters of J.R.R. Tolkien.*

If you are not familiar with this fire—it's difficult to keep up with how many we have in California—then here's a quick rundown of the pertinent information: it was the deadliest and most destructive wildfire in California's history, burning 153,336 acres, destroying 18,804 buildings, killing 85 people, and injuring 17 more. Over 52,000 people were evacuated, many of whom are still homeless today.

But tragedy is much more than facts and figures. It's real-life stories about real loss. While I didn't live in Paradise at the time, my best friend and author of the Foreword to this book, Michael Machuga, did. When he lost his home to the fire, we also lost our garden, orchard, and vineyard that we had spent a half a decade building. Here's how I describe the devastation in our book, *The Bonfire Sessions*:

> As you can see, we had a beautiful setting here in the Sierra Nevada foothills, and I say "had" because, if you aren't aware [...] the infamous Camp Fire wiped out just about everything. The lovely little grove of fruit trees in the south part of the property? Gone. The vineyard? Gone. The orchard smack-dab in the middle of the property? Gone. The garden? Gone. Even the compost—all of it—gone![183]

As you can probably tell by the lack of creativity in the writing, the pain was still all too palpable. Like Sam did when he discovered the felled Party Tree, I can still remember breaking down in tears as I wrote that paragraph mere months after the fire. I remember the heartache the first time I stepped foot onto the property, the numbing feeling that overtook my body as I walked across the scarred earth where a garden once proudly stood, the emptiness I felt when I realized our own Party Tree (affectionately known as the Piss Tree for what should be obvious reasons) had fallen. But also, like Sam, to this day I can still

....

183 Distefano and Machuga, *The Bonfire Sessions: Summer*, 7.

feel the motivation in my body from the trauma that came my way, as I continue doing my part in rebuilding what once was. Even though we can never replace what was lost, we can carry on its legacy in the new things we create in its stead, just as Sam did when he planted the Mallorn tree where the Party Tree once proudly stood.

In fact, as I write this, Michael and I will be coming up on our third season of the new garden. While we still miss the old property, I am happy to report that our new one is, to use Tolkien's word, "marvelous." On both the north and south ends of the property run lengthy blackberry hedges with the juiciest berries I have ever tasted. The vegetable garden, roughly three times the size of the original one, sits at the south end, at which the sloping land brings all the wonderful nutrients. Its fence is dotted with blueberries, both pink and blue fruiting species. Next to the garden is a variety of grapes that we one day hope to turn into a wine that is half as tasty as I imagine Old Winyards to be. And next to that is a new Piss Tree—an Autumn Blaze Maple currently standing ten feet tall. Along the south side are a handful of fruit trees—three peach, two cherry, two apple, two fig, two almond, with more to plant in the coming year. All in all, while the devastation cut deeply—nearly as deeply as Frodo's wound from the Morgul blade—it was not going to thwart us from scouring our own Shire deep in the heart of the Northern California foothills.

FINE FELLOWSHIP ALONG THE WAY

As we've done so many times throughout this book, we'll end the chapter with a word about friendship.

During the Scouring of the Shire, the love and affection our Hobbit friends have for their land is evident, but even more so is their love and affection for each other. They have been to *hell* and back—or in Frodo and Sam's case, *Mordor*—and have come out the other end closer with one another than they probably ever thought imaginable. Sure, each have suffered harm, no one more so than Frodo. But through it all, they have learned to lean on each other for strength and guidance. As every good Hobbit knows, this is exactly what it means to be good Hobbit—honest, true to their word, loyal to a fault.

The same holds true for Michael and me. Over the past four years, we have each suffered and lost much. Not only did we lose the garden, but he and his wife lost their home. On top of that, he went through the excruciating pain of a cancer diagnosis, subsequent radiation and chemotherapy, and multiple surgeries. And while he has come out the other side of it stronger and, thankfully, intact, life has been not without its difficulties. Through it all, we've been there for one another, relationally and spiritually. To this day, every week we continue to sit around a firepit, chatting about all the big ideas of life, smoking the finest pipe-weed we can get our hands on, eating fresh salsas made from our garden, and staring out and across the grass and creek and into the garden and beyond. And if that is not living the Hobbit life, I don't know what is. We have our fellowship, and though it is small, it is enough. In fact, like true Hobbits in all but size, it is *more than* enough—our very own Bag End, where fellowship grounds us to the earth beneath our feet, and where friendship blossoms like a bed of zinnias basking in the heat of the summer's sun.

POSTSCRIPT

the wisdom of hobbits

"It is no bad thing to celebrate a simple life."

— BILBO BAGGINS

Life can be complicated. It will move at the speed of light and yet we are all expected to be able to keep up, lest we want to drown (to mix metaphors). We are all too often bombarded by fast-talking advertisers, big-money corporations, and shifty-eyed politicians, rarely having time to slow down to smell the star jasmine. After reading this book, my hope is that that will change for you.

For me, writing *The Wisdom of Hobbits* has been a reminder of why I love this diminutive race so much. They are so simple yet so profound, so down to earth yet still savvy and philosophical in their own right—a perfect antidote to the chaos that comes with living in the twenty-first century. Not that we should recoil from society like a giant spider wounded by a humble dagger, but by applying the wisdom of Hobbits, we have a way to stay grounded amidst of the disorder and confusion of modern life. That is my hope, anyway.

My other hope is that because of reading about the wisdom of Hobbits, you'll fall deeper in love with Tolkien's writings, as I have after having written this little homage. In my mind, he is the greatest mythologist humanity has ever produced, his tales rivaling even that of the Christian and Jewish Scriptures. And in the midst of all his stories of valor, honor, bravery, and gallantry, it's not the biggest, baddest heroes who rise to the top. It's the little guys (and gals). It's the humble Hobbit who takes center stage, proving that it doesn't matter how big or how strong or how powerful you may think you are. *True power is in resisting it.* As Bilbo, Frodo, and Samwise show us, true power is found in pity, and mercy, and forgiveness. These are the things that save Middle-earth. Nothing more.

So, have hope that like our Hobbit friends, though your life may be wrought with peril, though it may be imbued with suffering, though it may seem like it's too often well out of your control, there may come a day where, like Sam, you can come home to your comfy chair and say, "Well, I'm back."[184] You, too, can enjoy your very own Shire, but only after doing the hard work of going on adventure. And while you never know where the Road will take you, have hope that you'll always have a safe place to come home to when you're done. Even if the adventures of life go awry, you can always regroup around the firepit at home. Whether that home is in a hole on Bagshot Row or in an apartment in Manhattan matters not; the spirit of the Shire is

....

184 Tolkien, *The Return of the King*, 340.

in sharing life with fellow Hobbits, sipping wine, smoking pipe-weed, eating rashers of bacon and mushrooms, and laughing and singing until our heart's content.

And now, I leave you with this, as its charm and simplicity encapsulate what it means to be the friend of a Hobbit. May your days be long, your gardens green, your songs jolly, and your feet furry. Until we meet on our next adventure …

> "For the Quest is achieved, and now all is over. I am glad you are here with me. Here at the end of all things, Sam."[185]

. . . .

185 Ibid., 241.

APPENDIX A

Various sketches from in and around the shire

FIGURE I: FIRESIDE FELLOWSHIP

FIGURE 2: BAG END, FRONT PORCH

FIGURE 3: POTATOES & CONIES

FIGURE 4: SOMEWHERE NEAR THE WATER

FIGURE 5: A HOBBIT GARDEN

FIGURE 6: A STROLL THROUGH THE MARISH

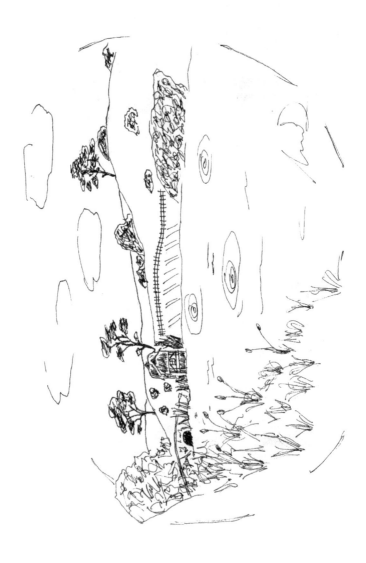

FIGURE 7: THE OLD MILL

APPENDIX B

maps: Bag end; hobbiton & bywater, the shire

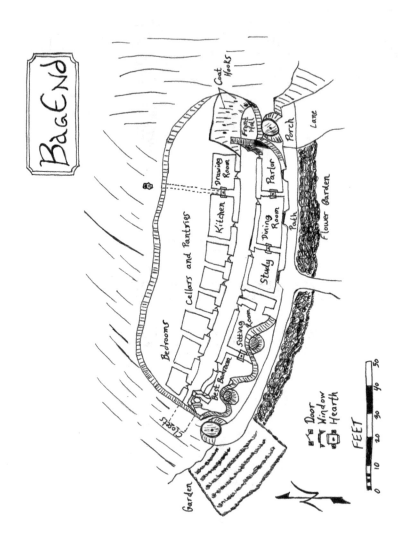

Bag End

Coat Hooks

Front Hall

Porch

Lane

Drawing Room

Parlor

Flower Garden

Kitchen

Dining Room

Path

Cellars and Pantries

Study

Bedrooms

Sitting Room

Best Bedroom

Closets

Garden

Door
Window
Hearth

FEET

0 10 20 30 40 50

FIGURE 1: BAG END

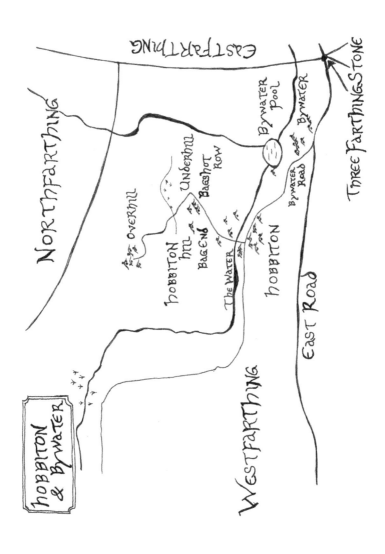

FIGURE 2: HOBBITON & BYWATER

APPENDIX C

A Survey of Various Crops, Flowers, Trees, and Shrubs Located in the Shire

The following crops and other plants either grow naturally, or are farmed/gardened in the Shire. There are certainly other plants—various shrubs, herbs, and flowers not mentioned by name[186]—but

. . . .

186   We can infer such things as caraway seed, given that Bilbo made seedcake for the Dwarves; hemp, since Hobbits were rope-makers; hops and grapes, given that ales and wines were brewed in the Shire; and all the various shrubs Frodo recognizes in Ithilien, such as tamarisks, pungent terebinth, junipers, myrtles, and bays. However, because these things are not mentioned explicitly, we can't know for sure which actually grew in the Shire, and which may have been imported from elsewhere.

instead of speculating which ones should be included, I have decided to include only those mentioned directly in the source material from J.R.R. Tolkien's Legendarium.

ALDER (*ALNUS*)

- Plant Type: Deciduous Tree
- Sun Exposure: Full Sun to Partial Shade
- Soil pH: Acidic to Slightly Acidic
- Hardiness Zones: 5–8
- Notes: Can grow up to 80 feet in height. Part of the birch family. Most leaves don't change color in the fall.

APPLE (MALUS DOMESTICA)

- Plant Type: Fruit Tree
- Sun Exposure: Full Sun
- Soil pH: Neutral
- Hardiness Zones: 3–8
- Notes: Harvest in fall. Comes in many varieties. Most need pollen from another tree in order to grow fruit. Requires yearly pruning.

ASH (*FRAXINUS*)

- Plant Type: Deciduous Tree
- Sun Exposure: Full Sun
- Soil pH: Acidic to Neutral

- Hardiness Zones: 2–9
- Notes: Grows to a towering 120 feet, depending on the variety. The wood has many purposes, including timber and tools.

BIRCH (*BETULA*)

- Plant Type: Deciduous Tree
- Sun Exposure: Full Sun; Partial Shade
- Soil pH: Acidic to Slightly Acidic
- Hardiness Zones: 2–7
- Notes: Has unique bark, which peels off in strips. A range of leaf colors, depending on the variety. Bright yellow in the fall.

BLACKBERRY (*RUBUS FRUTICOSUS*)

- Plant Type: Fruit Bush/Vine
- Sun Exposure: Full Sun
- Soil pH: Acidic
- Hardiness Zones: 4–10
- Notes: A hearty perennial, perfect for snacking or baked in pies and tarts. Can be invasive, so regular pruning is recommended. Likes plenty of moisture.

CABBAGE (*BRASSICA OLERACEA*)

- Plant Type: Vegetable

- Sun Exposure: Full Sun
- Soil pH: Neutral
- Hardiness Zones: 1–10
- Notes: A cool-season vegetable, perfect for spring or fall. Packed with vitamins, this leafy vegetable can be prepared in a number of ways.

CARROT (*DAUCUS CAROTA SUBSP. SATIVUS*)

- Plant Type: Vegetable
- Sun Exposure: Full Sun
- Soil pH: Neutral
- Hardiness Zones: 3–10
- Notes: Cool-season crop grown in spring. An excellent source of vitamin A. Can be served cooked or raw.

CHESTNUT (*CASTANEA*)

- Plant Type: Deciduous Tree
- Sun Exposure: Full Sun
- Soil pH: Acidic to Slightly Acidic
- Hardiness Zones: 4–9
- Notes: Can reach up to 100 feet in height. Reddish-brown or gray bark. The nut from the tree has many culinary uses, including being milled into flour for livestock.

CORN—BARLEY (*HORDEUM VULGARE*), RYE (*SECALE CEREALE*), WHEAT (*TRITICUM*), OATS (*AVENA SATIVA*)

- Plant Type: Cereal Grains
- Sun Exposure: Full Sun
- Soil pH: Slightly Acidic to Neutral
- Hardiness Zones: Varied, depending on the crop
- Notes: "Corn" in Middle-earth is a catch-all term that refers to various cereal crops, including barley, rye, wheat, and oats.

DAFFODIL (*NARCISSUS SPP.*)

- Plant Type: Flower
- Sun Exposure: Full Sun: Partial Shade
- Soil pH: Slightly Acidic to Neutral
- Hardiness Zones: 3–9
- Notes: One of the earliest spring-blooming flowers. Comes in orange, white, and yellow. Quite hardy and in most climates, can grow as a perennial.

ELM (*ULMUS*)

- Plant Type: Deciduous Tree
- Sun Exposure: Full Sun; Partial Shade
- Soil pH: Acidic to Neutral
- Hardiness Zones: 3–9

- Notes: Large shade trees with round, serrated leaves. Has a wide and extensive root system. Can grow up to six feet per year.

FIR (*ABIES*)

- Plant Type: Evergreen Tree
- Sun Exposure: Full Sun; Partial Shade
- Soil pH: Acidic to Slightly Acidic
- Hardiness Zones: 3–8
- Notes: Can live to be at least 500 years old. Typically, around 40 to 60 feet in height. Most varieties have cones that grow in an upright position.

HAZELNUT (*CORYLUS*)

- Plant Type: Deciduous Tree
- Sun Exposure: Full Sun
- Soil pH: Slightly Acidic
- Hardiness Zones: 4–8
- Notes: In the birch family. Several varieties produce nuts that can be used culinarily. Moderately shade tolerant and deep rooted.

LABURNUM (*LABURNUM*)

- Plant Type: Deciduous Tree
- Sun Exposure: Full Sun; Partial Shade

- Soil pH: Neutral to Alkaline
- Hardiness Zones: 5–7
- Notes: Grows up to 25 feet. Has smooth grey or olive-green bark. Produces bright yellow flowers, which bloom between May and June.

LILY (*LILIUM SPP.*)

- Plant Type: Flower
- Sun Exposure: Full Sun; Partial Shade
- Soil pH: Varies
- Hardiness Zones: 4–9
- Notes: Attracts butterflies. Flowers come in all colors, including orange, pink, purple, red, white, and yellow. Best to plant bulbs in late summer, or in early spring after the last frost.

LINDEN (*TILIA*)

- Plant Type: Deciduous Tree
- Sun Exposure: Full Sun; Partial Shade
- Soil pH: Neutral to Alkaline
- Hardiness Zones: 3–8
- Notes: Can be identified by their symmetrical growth habits. Some can live up to 1,000 years. Contains smooth grey bark and heart-shaped, asymmetrical leaves.

MALLORN (*MALINORNË*)

- Plant Type: Deciduous Tree
- Sun Exposure: Full Sun
- Soil pH: Unknown
- Hardiness Zones: Unknown
- Notes: A large tree that, until planted in Hobbiton, has only grown in Aman, Númenor, and Lórien. After their visit to Lothlórien, Galadriel gives Sam the nut of a Mallorn, which Sam plants in the Party Tree's place after it is felled by Saruman's forces. It becomes the first and only Mallorn outside of Lórien. Though deciduous, its golden leaves do not fall until spring, when they are replaced by the following year's blossoms.

MARJORAM (*ORIGANUM MAJORANA*)

- Plant Type: Herb
- Sun Exposure: Full Sun
- Soil pH: Acidic to Alkaline
- Hardiness Zones: 9–10 (perennial); 7–8 (partial perennial); 6 and colder (annual)
- Notes: Similar to oregano. Can be grown year-round in some climates. Used culinarily in both savory and sweet dishes.

MUSHROOM (*AGARICUS BISPORUS*)

- Plant Type: Edible Fungus

- Sun Exposure: Shade
- Soil pH: Slightly Acidic
- Hardiness Zones: 3–8
- Notes: Grown all throughout the Shire, especially in Farmer Maggot's fields. Used in many culinary dishes. Often given as parting gifts.

NASTURTIAN, NOW COMMONLY SPELLED "NASTURTIUM" (*TROPAEOLUM MAJUS*)

- Plant Type: Flower
- Sun Exposure: Full Sun; Partial Shade
- Soil pH: Slightly Acidic to Neutral
- Hardiness Zones: 10, 11
- Notes: An easy-to-grow flower. Comes in a variety of colors, including orange, red, white, and yellow. Attracts butterflies. Combines well with vegetables as it attracts pests, keeping them off edible crops.

ONION (*ALLIUM CEPA*)

- Plant Type: Vegetable
- Sun Exposure: Full Sun
- Soil pH: Neutral
- Hardiness Zones: Any
- Notes: Can be planted in either spring or fall. Tolerates frost. Likes well-drained soil. Comes in many varieties. Perfect for stews and soups.

PARTY TREE (*UNKOWN*)

- Plant Type: Deciduous Tree
- Sun Exposure: Full Sun
- Soil pH: Likely Acidic
- Hardiness Zones: Unknown
- Notes: A large tree (likely deciduous, though never actually identified in the text), south of Bag End in Hobbiton. Cut down under Saruman's orders during The Scouring of the Shire.

PARSLEY (*PETROSELINUM CRISPUM*)

- Plant Type: Herb
- Sun Exposure: Full Sun; Partial Shade (in warmer climates)
- Soil pH: Acidic to Slightly Acidic
- Hardiness Zones: 4–9
- Notes: Generally grown as an annual; can be grown as a biennial in some climates. Likes moist soil, but is fairly drought tolerant.

PINE (*PINUS*)

- Plant Type: Evergreen Tree
- Sun Exposure: Full Sun
- Soil pH: Acidic to Alkaline
- Hardiness Zones: 2–10

- Notes: Grows best in temperate to subtropical climates. Likes sandy or well-drained soil. Adapts well to dry conditions.

PLUM (*PRUNUS SPP.*)

- Plant Type: Fruit Tree
- Sun Exposure: Full Sun
- Soil pH: Slightly Acidic to Neutral
- Hardiness Zones: 3–9
- Notes: A type of stone fruit, similar to the peach and nectarine. Generally, needs a cross-pollinator. Can be used in jams, jellies, or as a snack, right off the tree.

POTATO (*SOLANUM TUBEROSUM*)

- Plant Type: Vegetable
- Sun Exposure: Full Sun
- Soil pH: Acidic
- Hardiness Zones: 3–10b
- Notes: Plant very early in the gardening season. Enjoy sunny, cooler weather and well-drained, loose soil. Likes consistent, even moisture.

RASPBERRY (*RUBUS*)

- Plant Type: Fruit Bush/Vine
- Sun Exposure: Full Sun

- Soil pH: Slightly Acidic to Neutral
- Hardiness Zones: 2–8
- Notes: An excellent source of vitamin C. Can be eaten right off the vine, or used in jams, pies, and tarts. Generally harvested in summer, with some varieties producing berries well into the fall.

ROWAN (*SORBUS SUBG. SORBUS*)

- Plant Type: Deciduous Tree
- Sun Exposure: Full Sun; Partial Shade
- Soil pH: Slightly Acidic to Neutral
- Hardiness Zones: 3–5
- Notes: Fast growing, characterized by its bright red berries at the end of summer. Greyish-brown bark that is smooth and shiny when wet.

SAGE (*SALVIA OFFICINALIS*)

- Plant Type: Herb
- Sun Exposure: Full Sun
- Soil pH: Slightly Acidic to Neutral
- Hardiness Zones: 5–8
- Notes: A versatile garden herb. A hardy perennial in most climates. Grows well with rosemary, cabbage, and carrots, but not cucumbers.

SNAPDRAGON (*ANTIRRHINUM*)

- Plant Type: Flower
- Sun Exposure: Full Sun; Partial Shade
- Soil pH: Slightly Acidic to Neutral
- Hardiness Zones: 7–11
- Notes: Comes in a variety of colors. Can be grown as an annual or as a perennial. Likes adequate watering and well-drained soil. A mainstay in all flower gardens.

STRAWBERRY (*FRAGARIA SPP.*)

- Plant Type: Fruit Bush/Vine
- Sun Exposure: Full Sun
- Soil pH: Slightly Acidic to Neutral
- Hardiness Zones: 2–10
- Notes: Easy to grow. Bears fruit at various times throughout the growing season, depending on the variety. Established plants will produce runners that will root and grow into new plants. Can be used in pies, jams, jellies, or eaten right off the vine.

SUNFLOWER (*HELIANTHUS ANNUUS*)

- Plant Type: Flower
- Sun Exposure: Full Sun
- Soil pH: Slightly Acidic to Slightly Alkaline
- Hardiness Zones: 4–9

- Notes: Bright blooms that last all summer. Heat-tolerant, pest-resistant, and attractive to pollinators. Seeds and oil are a good source of food.

SWEET GALENAS, AKA PIPE-WEED (*NICOTIANA TABACUM*)

- Plant Type: Herb
- Sun Exposure: Full Sun to Partial Shade
- Soil pH: Slightly Acidic
- Hardiness Zones: 2–10
- Notes: Grown in various locations throughout Middle-earth. Hobbits were the first to use it for smoking. Popular varieties include Longbottom Leaf, Old Toby, Southern Star, and Southlinch.

THYME (*THYMUS VULGARIS*)

- Plant Type: Herb
- Sun Exposure: Full Sun
- Soil pH: Slightly Acidic to Slightly Alkaline
- Hardiness Zones: 5–9
- Notes: A fantastic garden herb. Adds rustic savory flavors to soups, meats, and vegetables. A perennial evergreen in most climates.

TOMATO (*SOLANUM LYCOPERSICUM*)

- Plant Type: Vegetable

- Sun Exposure: Full Sun
- Soil pH: Acidic to Neutral
- Hardiness Zones: 4–11
- Notes: A staple in most gardens. Prefers deep watering. Can be used in countless ways, from sauces and stews, to salads and fresh off the vine.

TURNIP (*BRASSICA RAPA*)

- Plant Type: Vegetable
- Sun Exposure: Full Sun
- Soil pH: Slightly Acidic to Neutral
- Hardiness Zones: 2–9
- Notes: Cool-weather vegetable, grown in both spring and fall. Water thoroughly and consistently. Both roots and greens can be harvested. Can be enjoyed raw, baked, boiled, roasted, or mashed.

WILLOW (*SALIX*)

- Plant Type: Deciduous Tree
- Sun Exposure: Full Sun; Partial Shade
- Soil pH: Slightly Acidic
- Hardiness Zones: 4–10
- Notes: A deciduous tree often found near bodies of water. The leaves change color throughout the year, from green in the summer to yellow in the fall.

APPENDIX D

pROminent hoBBitS throughout hiStoRY

BILBO BAGGINS

Bilbo is the first Hobbit to become famous outside of the Shire, after his adventures with Gandalf, Thorin Oakenshield, and the others. He was born on September 22 in the year 2890 of the Third Age. His parents were Bungo Baggins and Belladonna Took.

FRODO BAGGINS

Frodo is arguably the most famous of all Hobbits after bearing the One Ring to the cracks of Mt. Doom, where it is destroyed. He was born on September 22 in the year 2968 of the Third Age. His parents were Drogo Baggins and Primula Brandybuck, though due to a tragic accident, he was raised by his uncle Bilbo.

SAMWISE "SAM" GAMGEE

Sam is the only member of the Fellowship of the Ring to remain with Frodo until the very end of their journey to Mt. Doom. He was born on April 6 in the year 2980 of the Third Age. He is married to Rose "Rosie" Cotton and together they have thirteen children: Elanor, Frodo, Rose, Merry, Pippin, Goldilocks, Hamfast, Daisy, Primrose, Bilbo, Ruby, Robin, and Tolman.

MERIADOC "MERRY" BRANDYBUCK

Merry is one of four Hobbits in the Fellowship of the Ring who will later become a Knight of Rohan. He is an heir to the Brandybucks of Brandy Hall, eventually becoming Master of Buckland. He was born in 2982 of the Third Age to Saradoc Brandybuck and Esmeralda Took. He has at least one son with his wife, Estella Bolger.

PEREGRIN "PIPPIN" TOOK

Pippin is the youngest Hobbit of the Fellowship of the Ring. After the War of the Ring, he becomes Thain of the Shire. He was born in the Spring of 2990 of the Third Age to Paladin Took II and Eglantine Banks. He has one son, Faramir, with his wife Diamond of Long Cleeve.

FREDEGAR "FATTY" BOLGER

Fatty is one of Frodo's closest friends, even helping him to leave the Shire with the One Ring. He was born in 2980 of the Third Age to Odovacar Bolger and Rosamunda Took. His sister, Estella, eventually marries Meriadoc Brandybuck.

ELANOR GARDNER

Elanor is the first child of Samwise Gamgee and Rosie Cotton. She was born on March 25, T.A. 3021, and is the only one of Sam's children that Frodo knows personally. In 1482 of the Shire Reckoning, her father will give to her the *Red Book of Westmarch* before he passes into the Undying Lands to join Frodo.

OTHO SACKVILLE-BAGGINS

Otho was born to Longo Baggins and Camellia Sackville in 2910 of the Third Age. Though he has Pipe-weed plantations in the Southfarthing, the land he desires more than anything was Bag End. Though he will die before he can take ownership of it, his wife, Lobelia eventually calls Bag End home, albeit for a brief time.

LOTHO SACKVILLE-BAGGINS

Lotho is the son of Otho and Lobelia Sackville-Baggins and, like his parents, is generally disliked in the Shire. During the War of the Ring, he sides with Saruman and supports him in taking over the Shire. He is killed by Saruman's servant Gríma Wormtongue prior to the return of Frodo, Sam, and the others.

LOBELIA SACKVILLE-BAGGINS

Like her husband Otho, Lobelia is known as a greedy Hobbit. However, unlike her son Lotho, she opposes Saruman and is eventually jailed in the Lockholes at Michel Delving. Devastated by the murder of her son, she gifts Bag End back to Frodo after their return from Mt. Doom.

GERONTIUS TOOK, AKA "OLD TOOK"

The Old Took is a famous Hobbit who was born in 2790 of the Third Age, dying some 130 years later. A friend of Gandalf, he is known for his raucous midsummer-eve parties, replete with food, drinks, and of course, fireworks.

BANDOBRAS "BULLROARER" TOOK

Bullroarer is most famous for his heroism during the Battle of Greenfields, leading a charge against invading goblins, whereby he knocked the goblin chief's head from his body, sending it a hundred yards and down into a nearby rabbit hole.

SMÉAGOL

Sméagol is a Stoorish Hobbit who, after "discovering" the One Ring, will later be known as Gollum due to the groveling noises he makes with his throat. A side-effect of carrying the Ring with him is that his life is extended far beyond any other Hobbits, dying at 589 years old but only after falling into the Cracks of Mt. Doom.

DÉAGOL

Déagol is the cousin and best friend of Sméagol, and first Hobbit to bear the Ring. However, shortly after its discovery, he is murdered by his cousin, who desires to have it as a birthday present.

FARMER MAGGOT

Maggot is a farmer who lives in the Marish region of the Shire's Eastfarthing. He is known for growing turnips, mushrooms, and poppies. Though he has had run-ins with a younger Frodo, the two will later become friends after Farmer Maggot aids Frodo, Sam, and Pippin in getting them across the Brandywine Bridge and away from the Black Riders that are searching for the Hobbits.

MRS. MAGGOT

Mrs. Maggot is the wife of Farmer Maggot. A hospitable Hobbit, she is best known for helping Frodo, Sam, and Pippin by gifting them a large basket of bacon and mushrooms before their journey to Bucklebury Ferry.

Bibliography

Amendt-Raduege, PhD, Amy. "A Seed of Courage: Merry, Pippin, and the Ordinary Hero." In *A Wilderness of Dragons: Essays in Honor of Verlyn Flieger*. Wayzata: The Gabbro Head Press, 2018.

Barth, Karl. *Church Dogmatics*. Translated by G.W. Bromiley, G.T. Thompson, and Harold Knight. London: T&T Clark, 2009.

Campbell, Joseph. *The Hero with A Thousand Faces*. Princeton: Princeton University Press, 1949.

Darnov, Doron. "'A Mind of Metal and Wheels': Technology, Instrumental Reason, and Industrialization in *The Lord of the Rings*." In *UC Berkeley Comparative Literature Undergraduate Journal*. Accessed May 9, 2022. https://ucbcluj.org/a-mind-of-metal-and-wheels-technology-instrumental-reason-and-industrialization-in-the-lord-of-the-rings/#_edn1.

Dickerson, Matthew T., and Evans, Jonathan D. *Ents, Elves, and Eriador: The Environmental Vision of J.R.R. Tolkien*. Lexington: University Press of Kentucky, 2006.

Distefano, Matthew J. "Reclaiming the Word 'Queer'." *Patheos.* (January 22, 2022). https://www.patheos.com/blogs/ allsetfree/2022/01/reclaiming-the-word-queer/.

Distefano, Matthew J., and Machuga, Michael. *The Bonfire Sessions: A Year of Shadow and Flame.* Oak Glen: Quoir, 2021.

———. *The Bonfire Sessions: Summer.* Oak Glen: Quoir, 2020.

Flieger, Verlyn. "Frodo and Aragorn: The Concept of the Hero." In *Understanding The Lord of the Rings: The Best of Tolkien Criticism.* Eds. Rose A Zimbardo and Neil D. Isaacs. New York: Houghton Mifflin, 2004, 122–45.

———. "The Curious Incident of the Dream of the Barrow: Memory and Reincarnation in Middle-earth." In *Tolkien Studies IV.* (2007): 99–112.

Friedman, Paul, and Anderson, Mark. "'What's Taters, Precious?': Food in Tolkien's 'The Lord of the Rings.'" *Imago Temporis, Medium Aevum,* VI (2012): 339–350.

Hart, David Bentley. *The Experience of God: Being, Consciousness, Bliss.* New Haven: Yale University Press, 2013.

———. "God, Creation, and Evil: The Moral Meaning of creation ex nihilo." *Radical Orthodoxy: Theology, Philosophy, Politics,* Vol. 3, Number 1 (September 2015):1–17.

Hopper, Elizabeth. "What Is the Contact Hypothesis in Psychology?" *ThoughtCo.* (October 26, 2019). https://www. thoughtco.com/contact-hypothesis-4772161.

Jackson, Peter, director. *The Hobbit: The Battle of the Five Armies.* 2014; New Line Cinema, 2014. 2 hr., 24 min. Blu-ray Disc, 1080p HD.

———. *The Hobbit: The Desolation of Smaug.* 2013; New Line Cinema, 2013. 2 hr., 41 min. Blu-ray Disc, 1080p HD.

———. *The Hobbit: An Unexpected Journey.* 2012; New Line Cinema, 2012. 2 hr., 49 min. Blu-ray Disc, 1080p HD.

———. *The Lord of the Rings: The Fellowship of the Ring.* 2001; New Line Cinema, 2001. 2 hr., 58 min. Blu-ray Disc, 1080p HD.

———. *The Lord of the Rings: The Return of the King.* 2003; New Line Cinema, 2003. 4 hr., 11 min. Blu-ray Disc, 1080p HD.

———. *The Lord of the Rings: The Two Towers.* 2002; New Line Cinema, 2002. 2 hr., 59 min. Blu-ray Disc, 1080p HD.

Kant, Immanuel. *Religion Within the Limits of Reason Alone.* Translated by Theodore M. Greene and Hoyt H. Hudson. New York: Harper & Row, 1960.

Linning, Stephanie. "Bombed but not beaten: Amazing merged photographs show the damage done to Britain's streets during WWI air raids and how they look 100 years later." *Daily Mail.* (August 14, 2014). https://www.dailymail.co.uk/news/article-2724769/The-original-Blitz-Amazing-photographs-damage-Britain-WW1-air-raids-look-100-years-later.html.

Murphy, Brian. "Free Will in Tolkien's *The Lord of the Rings*: Choice and Persuasion in a Fine Balance." *The Silver Key.* (August 25, 2008). https://thesilverkey.blogspot.com/2008/08/free-will-in-tolkiens-lord-of-rings.html.

Niiler, Lucas. "Green Reading: Tolkien, Leopold and the Land Ethic." In *Journal of the Fantastic in the Arts*. 10 (3): 276–85.

_____. "Timely, again: Tolkien's Fantastic Ecology." In *Academic Exchange Quarterly*. (December 22, 2003.) https://www.thefree library.com/Timely%2c+again%3a+Tolkien%27s+fantastic+ ecology.-a0114168071.

Rohr, Richard. *Breathing Under Water: Spirituality and the Twelve Steps*. Cincinnati: St. Anthony Messenger, 2011.

Shippey, Tom. *The Road to Middle-Earth: How J.R.R. Tolkien Created a New Mythology*. New York: Houghton Mifflin, 2003.

Sisto, Alan. "Túrin: 'Simple Twist of Fate,' or "Freewill." *Prancing Pony Ponderings*. (April 30, 2017). https:// theprancingponypodcast.com/2017/04/30/ turin-simple-twist-of-fate-or-freewill/.

Tolkien, J.R.R. "Athrabeth Finrod Ah Andreth." From *The History of Middle-earth: Boxed Set*. New York: William Morrow, 2020.

———."Of Dwarves and Men." From *The Peoples of Middle-earth: The History of Middle-earth*. Edited by Christopher Tolkien. Boston: Houghton Mifflin-Harcourt, 1996.

———. *The Hobbit*. New York: Del Rey, 1996.

———. *The Lord of the Rings: The Fellowship of the Ring*. New York: Ballantine, 1993.

———. *The Lord of the Rings: The Return of the King*. New York: Ballantine, 1993.

————. *The Lord of the Rings. The Two Towers*. New York: Ballantine, 1993.

————. *The Silmarillion*. New York: Ballantine, 1999.

————. *The Letters of J.R.R. Tolkien*. Edited by Humphrey Carpenter. Boston: Houghton-Mifflin-Harcourt, 1981.

Tolkien, J.R.R., and Tolkien, Christopher. *Unfinished Tales*. Boston: Houghton Mifflin, 1980.

Waito, David M. "The Shire Quest: The 'Scouring of the Shire' as the Narrative and Thematic Focus." In *Mythlore* 28:3/4, Spring/Summer 2010: 155–178.

Williams, Donald T. *Mere Humanity: G.K. Chesterton, C.S. Lewis, and J.R.R. Tolkien on the Human Condition*. Nashville: Broadman & Holman, 2006.

For more information about Matthew J. Distefano,

or to contact him for speaking engagements,

please visit *www.AllSetFree.com*

Many voices. One message.

For more information, please visit

www.quoir.com

CPSIA information can be obtained
at www.ICGtesting.com
Printed in the USA
BVHW080531230323
660939BV00003B/187